THE BRONC BUSTER

Tormented by a fearsome gang because of his small stature, fourteen-year-old Ian Hennessy swears one day never to run from anyone again. Years later, as the young bronc buster stares down a gunfighter, there is no doubt that his old enemy — Shaunnessy O'Toole, ringleader of his childhood bullies — is behind it. Meanwhile, a second man lurks nearby, also poised to shoot. All Hennessy's dreams — establishing a ranch, marrying the girl he loves — hang in the balance of this moment . . .

BILLY HALL

THE BRONC BUSTER

Complete and Unabridged

LINFORD
Leicester

First published in Great Britain in 2013 by
Robert Hale Limited
London

First Linford Edition
published 2015
by arrangement with
Robert Hale Limited
London

A catalogue record for this book is available
from the British Library.

ISBN 978–1–4448–2572–5

Published by
F. A. Thorpe (Publishing)
Anstey, Leicestershire

Set by Words & Graphics Ltd.
Anstey, Leicestershire
Printed and bound in Great Britain by
T. J. International Ltd., Padstow, Cornwall

This book is printed on acid-free paper

1

Escape! Get away! Run!

Ian Hennessy could think of nothing else. His eyes darted about desperately, seeking an avenue that offered any chance to flee impending disaster.

Ranged in front of him were two of his most feared tormenters. The other two of the foursome were behind him. He was hemmed in. Any one of them would have been more than a match for Ian. To face the four together was unthinkable.

The leader of the four was Shaunnessy O'Toole. That both he and Ian were Irish seemed as unlikely as snow in July. Shaunnessy was big, even at fourteen. Ian could have passed for ten or eleven, though they were actually the same age. Shaunnessy was red-headed, blue-eyed and fair skinned, liberally freckled, with a broad face and coarse features. His broad shoulders and thick chest already demanded a shirt too large for many grown men. Ian's dark hair curled around his fine features and dark eyes, making him look even smaller than he was.

For weeks now Ian had employed every wile he could conceive to get out of school and make it home before Shaunnessy and his friends could catch him. Sometimes it was pure speed. Ian would burst out the door of the one-room school house at the first syllable of the teacher's dismissal, running full tilt by the time he hit the bottom of the steps. From there it was a simple matter to outrun the others. He could outrun nearly anybody.

He loved to run, when it wasn't a necessity. He would often run across the hills near the burgeoning town of Sioux City just for the thrill of it. He thought he could run from sunup to sundown without tiring. His feet fairly flew across the hills and valleys, wind blowing in his hair, arms pumping in time with his feet, his whole being ecstatic with the freedom and sensation of speed.

There was no freedom at school. Even at recess, he was not allowed to leave the school yard. There Shaunnessy and his tag-along tormenters could harass him at will. They willed to do so every time the teacher's back was turned.

There was only so much they could do to him on the school grounds, though. It was never very long before the teacher's gaze would spot their efforts. Even so, they managed to punch him in the stomach, so no bruise would show, two or three times nearly every day. On occasion, if he was pretty sure the teacher wasn't watching, Shaunnessy would walk up like he was going to say something to Ian, then abruptly knee him in the groin. Then he and his friends would laugh and mock while Ian doubled up on the ground, sometimes vomiting from the intensity of the pain.

If the teacher noticed, she never said anything. Ian had long ago decided the teacher was as afraid of the quartet as he was.

Once in a while one of the four would manage to block his quick exit at the end of school. Then he would either have to try to stay after school and out-wait the quartet, or try to dodge around the one blocking his escape.

One warm spring day he had slid out an open window, but the teacher spotted him. He didn't respond to her command to 'Get back in here!' so he was paddled in front of the rest of the school the next day.

Most of the time his tormenters waited off the school grounds if they got out the door first, so the teacher didn't see what was happening.

That's what occurred today. Ian thought he had circled around far enough to give them the slip. He hadn't. Now he was trapped. Two of them were behind him. The other two were in front.

Ian took a quick step to his left. Even as all four of his enemies moved to block his way, he ducked back the other way and sprinted off. The hand of one of the four brushed across his shoulder, then he was clear. The others gave chase, but they already knew it was hopeless. Ian was far too fast for them to catch him, and they knew it.

Even so, Ian ran at top speed, heading down Nebraska Street, towards home. He flashed across Seventh Street, dodged horses, buggies and pedestrians, crossed Eighth Street, then was abruptly stopped by Everett Stinson. Everett owned a hardware store and gun shop just past Eighth Street on Nebraska Street. He might have been the only citizen of Sioux City who was aware of the ongoing torment of young Ian.

He had first noticed Ian pass his store in full flight a couple weeks previous. He began to watch, about time for school to be dismissed, and figured out quickly what was going on. Today he decided he had watched long enough.

Ian tried to dodge around the shopkeeper, but Everett was too quick on his feet. He wrapped his arms around the terrified boy and refused to let him pass.

'Lemme go!' Ian demanded, his voice betraying his fear.

'Just hold your horses,' Everett ordered in a firm but calm, soothing voice. 'They ain't chasin' you no more.'

Ian whirled and looked, sure his pursuers were not far behind. They were nowhere in sight.

He turned back, looking at the merchant in confusion.

'You ain't got a pa, do you, boy?'

Ian's eyes grew guarded at once. Hesitantly he said, 'No, sir.'

'What happened to your pa?'

'He got kilt in the war.'

'I figured as much. You got any brothers or sisters?'

'No, sir. Just me'n Ma.'

'Your mother takes in washing, doesn't she?'

'Yessir. That an' cleans houses for folks.'

'The O'Toole boy's been giving you a pretty hard time, ain't he?'

Ian hesitated a long while, before he said, 'Why?'

'I been noticin'. They kinda got you by the short hairs, don't they?'

'I don't know what that means.'

'They got you buffaloed, don't they?'

Ian hesitated again. Finally he said, 'There's four of 'em.'

'Yeah, I noticed. They're pretty big, too.'

'Yeah. Mean.'

'Cowards.'

'What?'

'They're cowards.'

Ian's voice conveyed the bitterness that roiled deep within him. 'Maybe you ain't noticed, mister, but I'm the one what's always runnin'.'

'That's why I stopped you.'

'Why?'

7

'To tell you to stop running.'

Ian looked at him as if this stranger had just ordered him to fly. 'If I stop runnin' they'll beat the snot outa me. Again.'

'And if you keep running, they'll catch you every once in a while, and beat the snot out of you every time they catch you.'

Ian studied the man, somehow intrigued, even though he'd already decided the guy was crazy. After a bit he said, 'So what'm I s'posed to do?'

'That's why I stopped you. I want to tell you exactly what to do.'

'What?'

'The O'Toole boy is the ringleader of the bunch, isn't he?'

'Yeah.'

'OK. Then tomorrow, you walk out of school like you don't have a care in the world.'

'Yeah, right! Then there's no way in the world I'll avoid 'em.'

'I don't want you to avoid them.'

'You want me to get beat up?'

'I want them to stop bullying you.'

'They ain't gonna stop bullyin' me by me lettin' 'em beat on me.'

'So listen to what I'm saying. Tomorrow, you walk out of school like you don't have a care in the world. As soon as you get out of sight of the school, they'll be waiting for you, right?'

'Right.'

'OK. You walk straight up to the O'Toole boy — what's his name?'

'Shaunnessy.'

'OK. You walk straight up to Shaunnessy, and you hit him just as hard and fast as you can, right on the nose.'

'Are you crazy? He'll kill me.'

As if he hadn't been interrupted, Everett said, 'You hit him right on the nose, just as hard as you can, then hit him in the stomach, hard, before he can react, then hit him in the face again, just as hard as you can hit.'

'Then he'll beat me up good!'

'Yes, he will. But if you watch, you can probably dodge and duck, so he'll have a hard time hitting you. You're awfully quick. So keep ducking, but most of all keep hitting him just as much as you can, just as hard as you can.'

'You want me to get beat up?'

'You're getting beat up already, aren't you?'

'Yeah. Sometimes.'

'So it won't be any different, except that you'll keep hitting him, as much as you can, as often as you can, as hard as you can. And don't forget to kick. Kick him in the shins or in the knees. If he grabs you in a bear hug, try to hit him in the nose with your forehead. If someone grabs you from behind, try to hit them in the nose with the back of your head. Or stomp on their toes, just as hard as you can. If somebody's holding you, poke them in the eye with your finger. Hard.'

'Oh, man, I'd love to do that, mister. But they'd work me over good.'

'Yeah, they probably will. But you'll live.'

Ian thought about it for a while. 'I lived through it afore.'

'And you can live through it again. Then let me tell you what happens next.'

'There's something comin' next?'

'You bet. And you're going to cause it. The next day, either before or after school, you go looking for them, if they're not waiting for you.'

'On purpose, go lookin' for them?'

'You bet. And you do the same thing. You don't say a word. You just walk up to Shaunnessy, and you hit him just as hard as you can hit. And you keep hitting as hard and fast as you can hit. And if they grab you, you hit and kick and scratch and gouge at their eyes, and everything you can think of that'll hurt. There's four of them, and only one of you, so forget about trying to fight fair. If you're in a fight, you need to hurt the other guy, or guys, just as much as you can, any way you can, just as fast as you can. If you get a chance to kick or knee any of them in the crotch, you do it,

11

just as hard as you can.'

'Then they'll beat up on me again.'

'Yeah, they will.'

'How many times do you want me gettin' beat up?'

'I'm guessing it will only take twice. Three at the most. Then I'll tell you what will happen. After the second or third time, when they see you coming, they'll start getting out of your way. They only chase you because you run from them. When they find out that it's going to hurt them to pick on you, they'll stop doing it. They're cowards. All four of them. That's why they always stay together, and why they always find someone littler than they are to pick on. But you don't have to be a victim: you can stand up to them.'

Clearly Ian was intrigued by the idea of standing up to the hated quartet. Just as clearly, he was terrified of trying to do so. Finally he said, 'You gonna be somewhere's that you can keep 'em from killin' me?'

Everett thought about it for a long

moment. Then he said, 'Yeah, I'll do that, son. I'll be where I can see what's going on. But don't count on me stepping in. I don't want to have to. If I have to step in, it won't be you standing up to them. They'll just watch for a chance when they know I'm not around. I'll keep them from doing you any lasting damage, but I won't stop them from beating up on you.'

'What about my ma?'

'What about your ma?'

'She don't want me fightin'. She gets all upset when they catch me an' bloody me up some. She'd be plumb mad if she knowed I started it this time.'

Everett pondered his words for a while. 'I'll tell you what I'll do. My wife and I will go over and talk to her tomorrow, while you're in school. I think I can convince her that it's what you have to do.'

After a long silence Ian said, 'I'll think on it some.'

As Ian started to walk on, Everett

said, 'Even if your ma don't agree, it's still going to be the only thing that'll ever stop those four. She might be pretty mad at both of us for a while. Women don't much understand the way of men, as a rule. That makes it kinda hard for a woman to teach a boy how to be a man.'

Instead of answering, Ian turned and walked toward home.

2

He thought the school day would never end. His stomach had been tied in a tight knot for the whole night. He was scarcely able to eat breakfast. His heart hammered incessantly. He had never had so much trouble concentrating on his lessons.

Four times during the day the teacher had snapped at him, reminding him to stop staring out the window. Each time, red-faced, his ears burning, he had buried his face in his book, only to get through less than a paragraph before his mind wandered again.

Some time during the night he had reconciled himself to taking a beating today. He knew what the store keeper had said was true. It was far more painful to live in constant fear than to face the fears and take whatever came.

He had mentally rehearsed the

actions he intended to take. He knew exactly where the quartet of bullies would be waiting for him, just out of sight of the school grounds. He could see them in his mind's eye, two of the four ranged across his path. There would almost certainly be one on either side and behind him, to prevent his ducking away and running.

One of those facing him would certainly be O'Toole. He was the leader. His leer would be smeared across his accursed face in anticipation of the things he had planned to do to Ian that day.

He had no way to know that Ian wasn't going to run today. He would walk swiftly to the big boy, and without any pause, without saying anything, would put everything he had into a straight right fist into the nose of his nemesis. As quickly as ever he could, he would follow that straight right with a left hook on to his cheekbone. That way, if he didn't get in another lick in the fight, O'Toole would sport a good black eye for several days.

Beyond that, he didn't know how to plan what to do. He had never tried to stand and fight before. He could fantasize those first couple of blows, and assume O'Toole would be startled enough at the first contact that he could get in at least one more blow before he reacted. After that, all bets were off.

He had tried to figure out what the other three would do, and how quickly they would do it. If they didn't react quickly enough, he might be able to bloody a nose or two on them as well. Then, when one of them managed to grab him from behind, as they liked to do so well, he had mentally practiced some of the things Everett Stinson had suggested. He just didn't know if he could actually do any of those things.

His distracted state of mind didn't go unnoticed by his four antagonists. They exchanged grins and meaningful glances every time he got reprimanded. They were certain it was fear of them that had driven him to that state of distraction.

When school was finally dismissed, he lingered a few minutes, instead of sprinting to the door as usual. The other four, to the contrary, dashed out the door the instant the teacher gave the word. Looking over their shoulders, they hurried out of sight.

Ian secured the leather strap around the books he was taking home with him. He made sure it was tight enough he could drop it without the books scattering. Carrying it loosely in his left hand, he walked out the door and down the steps. As he expected, Shaunnessy and company were nowhere in sight.

He strode swiftly, purposefully, toward home. He was no sooner out of sight of the school yard than he spotted Shaunnessy and Stanford King. They stood, exactly as he had pictured in his mind, directly in his path. From the corners of his eyes he spotted Milton McCormish and Glen Hidabrecht pacing him, staying far enough behind to block his ability to turn back.

His heart was pounding in his ears with a pulsing, rushing sound. He suddenly wanted to grin with an exuberance he could never remember. He resisted the urge to run at the pair before him, keeping his pace steady and even.

As he approached, Shaunnessy grinned. He spread his legs and put his hands on his hips. 'Well, look at what we have walkin' down the road, now would you?' he taunted.

Ian didn't answer. He didn't slow or swerve. He continued to walk directly toward the person he most feared in the world. As he approached, Shaunnessy's grin faded slightly. His eyes took on a slightly confused look. He couldn't remember Ian looking him in the eyes that way before.

When he thought he was just the right distance, Ian dropped the books he was carrying in his left hand, even as his right, the fist balled as tightly and hard as he could, barreled through the air and landed with a 'splat' on Shaunnessy's nose. Blood flew in all directions.

O'Toole was knocked backward a step, and hadn't begun to catch his balance when Ian's left hook landed solidly on his right cheekbone. Lights flashed and danced in his eyes.

Ian felt as if he had just been freed from tethers that had bound him since he could remember. He could smell the blood that was pouring from Shaunnessy's nostrils. He whirled to the side and planted a swift right then a left into the face of Stanford King. The startled would-be bully yelped in pain and surprise and took several quick steps backward.

Shaunnessy had already recovered from his shock and surprise and was running at Ian, fists balled. Instead of turning away, Ian stepped to meet him. He landed four fast, hard punches to the bigger boy's face, then instinctively ducked under the wild hay-maker right that Shaunnessy looped at him.

Even as he did, some instinct made him whirl to meet the onrush of the two who were stationed to keep him from running away. He managed to bloody the noses of both of them before they could react to his attack.

All four then converged on him in a rush. Having never been faced with an effort on Ian's part before, they badly underestimated his speed and quickness. He ducked low and dodged away, causing the four to collide with each other. As they staggered backward from the impact of their collision, Ian swung with all his might at the nearest one to him. His fist connected with the hinge of Milton's jaw. He collapsed to the ground as if he had been shot.

With a roar of outrage, Shaunnessy surged forward. Ian sidestepped and caught the big fellow on the ear with a stinging right as he passed, knocking him to the ground.

A pair of arms wrapped around Ian from behind, pinning his arms to his side. In a move he had practiced a dozen times in his mind the night before, Ian pressed back against the other's grip instead of pulling away. He snapped his head backward as hard as he could, gratified by the feel of his head contacting his captor's chin. The arms slackened slightly for the slightest moment, then tightened again.

Ian lifted a foot and stomped as hard as he could on the other boy's foot. The boy let out a howl of pain and released his hold, just as Stanford let loose with a hard right aimed at Ian's face. As Ian dodged, the fist grazed the side of his face and spent most of its energy splitting the skin just above Glen's right eye. Blood poured from the cut, blurring his vision.

Another pair of arms instantly grabbed Ian from behind. He tried to head butt the one holding him, but the same trick didn't work twice. When he lifted a foot to stomp on the toe, a fist connected with his face before he could bring it down.

Stars danced in Ian's eyes. A rushing, roaring sound filled his ears. Everything before him turned to a shade of red. He was unaware that the roaring yell he heard was issuing from his own throat. Like a thing possessed, he twisted, jerked, kicked and flailed, suddenly wrenching himself loose from the grip of the one trying to hold him.

He launched himself at the three who were still standing, swinging his fists and kicking as if he had completely lost his mind.

The numbers, however, were too great for even his wild rage to overcome. Blow after blow connected from all directions, until the world around him began to spin. He felt himself land prone on the ground and tried to rise. A booted foot caught him in the stomach, lifting him momentarily. He landed in a tight curl, doubled over tightly, fighting to gain a breath.

From some place far away he heard a frantic voice say, 'Somebody's comin'.'

Another voice said, 'Let's get outa here.'

A wave of blackness settled over him. He fought it back, forcing his lungs to suck in air. He lifted his head. Through a red blur he saw his four antagonists fleeing, two of them holding up a still unsteady Milton.

He forced himself to his hands and knees. Fighting his body's determination to double forward, he staggered to his feet. Unaware his fists were still tightly clenched, he watched the four out of sight.

'That's as fine a job of one against four as I've ever seen,' a voice behind him said.

Ian spun around. It was the wrong thing to do. The world didn't stop turning when he did. He staggered sideways, trying to catch his balance. A strong arm around his shoulders steadied him. 'Better take it easy for a few minutes,' the same voice advised.

'Gosh, that felt good,' Ian heard himself say. Even as he said it, he thought it was the most stupid thing anybody had ever said.

Everett Stinson laughed aloud. 'I bet it did at that,' he agreed. 'You aren't going to feel nearly as good after a bit, though.'

'I ain't never runnin' from nobody again, as long as I live,' Ian surprised himself again.

'I suspect that's true,' Everett agreed. 'Let's go over to the store and see if we can get you cleaned up a little.'

It took more than a little. By the time they were finished, Ian's face was swollen painfully. The half-dozen cuts stopped bleeding pretty quickly. His rib cage was well-bruised, and his stomach hurt a lot where Shaunnessy's boot had lifted him from the ground. One eye was swelled almost shut, but the cold, wet rag the shopkeeper held against it felt good.

An hour later, when Everett walked him home, Ian felt more alive than he could ever remember feeling. There was scarcely a part of his body that didn't hurt, but inside, the hurt that had been there as long as he could remember was gone.

His mother gasped when she opened the door and saw him. Everett quickly said, 'Mrs Hennessy, your son did himself proud today. He gave every one of the four bullies who have been picking on him a good deal more than they were able to give him. You have every right to be proud of him.'

'Ian, you look terrible!' she exclaimed, ignoring the merchant.

'I'm fine, Ma,' Ian grinned crookedly, through grossly swollen lips. 'I stood up to 'em, Ma. I got in some real good licks, an' I ain't never runnin' from 'em again. Nor nobody else. Not ever.'

It was clear from her expression that Nora Hennessy did not share any of his newfound enthusiasm.

3

Ian groaned aloud as he turned over in bed. Pain ripped through every part of his body. He grimaced at the pain, and the grimace induced additional pain in his face. He tried vainly to open his left eye, but the best he could manage was a tiny slit. The other eye opened OK, but his face was puffy around it. His lips were three times their normal thickness.

His stomach muscles screamed in protest as he sat up in bed. His mother stood over him, worry etched across her face. 'Are you all right, Ian?'

He grinned in spite of the pain it engendered. 'I'm fine, Ma,' he lied. 'A wee bit sore, 'tis true, but I'll be fine with a couple o' flapjacks an' eggs.'

His mother sighed deeply and shook her head. 'Men!' she said.

In spite of the disdain of the word, he heard the undertone of pride in her voice that she would never admit. 'She called me a man,' Ian thought.

With effort he got dressed. By the time he had done so and laced his boots, he was already beginning to feel better. He knew his face must be a sight, but he didn't care in the least.

He ate hurriedly, picked up his books and headed for the door.

''Tis a bit early to be leavin' for school,' his mother protested.

'Sure, I've got to see a fella or two before I get to school today,' he said.

He ducked out the door before she could ask any further questions. He dropped the Irish accent he knew his mother favored as he left the yard.

He knew from long and fearful observation the exact route followed by each of the four who had bedevilled him for so long. In the hour it took for the pain to subside enough for him to sleep the night before, he had devised a plan. It was, at the very least, a bold and daring one. Especially for him. It ran directly against everything that had become the habit of his life.

Walking quickly in the wrong direction to get to school, he encountered Glen Hidabrecht less than a block from home, just leaving for school. He noticed at once the evidence of the work his own fists had done the afternoon before. Without a word he delivered a straight right to Glen's face, bloodying his nose and knocking him flat.

Glen's astonishment turned to fright instantly. He rolled to his hands and knees, scrambled to his feet, and fled as fast as his feet could carry him. Ian grinned and watched him out of sight. Then he turned and headed on a path to intercept Milton McCormish. Milton saw him coming. His hand went involuntarily to his jaw, that hurt mightily every time he opened his mouth. He held up a hand, palm outward, toward the advancing object of his sudden fear. His eyes darted around as if trying in vain to find the three friends with whom he stayed in close company. There was nobody around, except him and a very determined-looking Ian Hennessy. He hesitated a moment longer, then turned tail and ran.

Everett Stinson's words ran through Ian's mind as if hearing the shopkeeper aloud. 'Cowards. They're all cowards. That's why they only bother you when they're all together.'

Too elated to feel the effects of yesterday's beating, Ian hurried to intercept Stanford King. Stanford, or Stan as he was known at school, reacted differently. He had a black eye and a swollen lip, and an angry scowl. As soon as he spotted Ian, he turned toward him. The two met, and both wordlessly took up the fight of the day before. Ian proved to be a great deal quicker than his adversary. He planted a hard left hook on Stan's nose and ducked under the round-house right that Stan had intended to dispatch Ian. Ian came in behind it with two swift blows to the bigger boy's face. He hoped they hurt Stan as much as they hurt his sore fists.

The two stood toe to toe for almost two minutes. Stan landed enough blows to bring back the ringing roar in Ian's ears. The metallic taste of his own blood tangy in his mouth, Ian once again fought like something possessed. Even so, he managed to duck and dodge the bulk of the other's punches. Almost all of his own landed solidly.

The end of the furious exchange was marked by Stan staggering back a step and lifting both hands. 'Nuff!' he said. 'I've had enough!'

'You sayin' 'Uncle'?' Ian demanded.

After only the briefest hesitation Stan said, 'Yeah. Uncle. I'm whipped. You win.'

Without wasting any further words, Ian turned and headed toward his planned interception with his chief antagonist. He had to wait a few minutes, as Shaunnessy was unaccustomedly late. The two boys spotted each other at almost the same moment.

Shaunnessy stopped and hesitated for the barest instant, then picked up his pace, heading directly toward Ian.

As he approached, Ian admired his handiwork on the much larger boy. Shaunnessy's nose was badly swollen and bright red. The brow above his left eye was swollen and sported a large scab that was left to keep it from starting to bleed again. The other eye was swollen as nearly shut as Ian's own, and deeply purple and brown. It was as fine a shiner as Ian had remembered seeing, but assumed his own would look as bad if he had bothered with a mirror.

Like his own, Shaunnessy's lips were heavily swollen. His uncertainty was telegraphed by his rapidly changing expression. For a moment it looked as if he were about to break into his customary taunting leer, then his face would grow cautious.

He finally opted for his instinctive assurance of his physical superiority. He stopped and planted his feet, hands on his hips. 'Well now, and ain't the little pipsqueak a sight this mornin'?' he said. 'Needin' a bit more o' the same now are ye?'

Once again, without a word, Ian continued his approach until he was at the desired distance, and once again put every ounce of strength he had into a straight right to the already swollen nose of his redheaded nemesis. Shaunnessy howled in pain and anger, and reacted with a surprisingly swift right that caught Ian directly on his left ear.

Ian was knocked sprawling. Shaunnessy stepped forward to kick the smaller boy while he was down, but Ian was too quick. He rolled to one side as his assailant's foot sailed past, narrowly missing his midriff. Thrown off balance by the failure of the expected resistance of the other's body, Shaunnessy staggered backward a step.

Instead of getting to his feet, Ian rolled over and from a prone position sent a foot as hard as he could into the side of Shaunnessy's knee. Once again the larger boy howled in pain and went to the ground.

Ian leaped to his feet, and instead of pressing his advantage, waited for the other boy to stand up as well.

As he did, Shaunnessy lunged forward, arms outstretched to tackle Ian. The move was totally unexpected and caught Ian moving forward. The weight and momentum of the bigger boy bore him backward and to the ground, the other's weight driving the wind from him as they landed.

Shaunnessy remained astride Ian, driving his right fist downward as hard as he could. Ian twisted to the side just enough for Shaunnessy's fist to graze his cheek and smash into the rock-hard ground. For the third time, the stronger boy howled in pain.

In a move he had neither thought of nor planned, Ian reached up and shoved two fingers into Shaunnessy's terribly painful nose, one into either nostril. He pulled and twisted, showering himself and the rusty-haired adversary with blood.

Shaunnessy rolled off of Ian, howling, trying desperately to relieve the excruciating pain inflicted on his already savaged nose.

Ian sent a knee into Shaunnessy's mid-section and scrambled to his feet. As he came to his own feet, Shaunnessy launched a looping left that caught Ian squarely on the jaw. Lights flashed in his head and the darkness reached up and pulled him into its oblivion instantly. He didn't even feel himself hit the ground.

Shaunnessy lifted a foot to kick the unconscious boy, then caught a movement from the corner of his eye. He looked around quickly. They were close enough to the school that other children were in the area. Several had stopped to watch the unexpected entertainment.

Walking as straight as he could, Shaunnessy headed toward the school, brushing as much of the dirt from his clothes as he could as he walked.

Moments later stabbing pain brought

consciousness back to Ian. He forced himself to roll over and scramble to his feet. Staggering and wobbly, he looked around for the other boy, only to realize he had already left. He took a deep, ragged breath.

'Are you OK, Ian?' a deeply concerned voice at his side asked.

He turned and looked into the worried eyes of Coralee Hickson, a schoolmate. 'Yeah, I'm fine, Corky,' he lied.

'You don't look fine at all,' she argued. 'You look beat up something awful. That must hurt a lot.'

'Not as much as runnin' away like I been doin',' he asserted.

She started to answer, then closed her mouth. She looked him up and down. 'We'd best get you to the pump at the school and get you cleaned up some,' she opined. 'Miss Hodges won't even let you stay at school looking like that.'

She grabbed him by the hand and started for the school grounds. Not knowing what else to do, he let her lead him to the pump behind the school house. From a pocket someplace she produced a small handkerchief. She plied the handle of the pump until water began to gush forth from the spout, then quickly soaked the handkerchief before the flow of water stopped.

'This is going to hurt,' she announced, as she began to wash the dirt and blood from his face. It did. At the same time, for reasons he didn't really understand, it felt good. It felt really good. He willed himself to neither groan nor grimace as Coralee scrubbed away all the signs of the fight of which the handkerchief was capable. Several times she ordered him to 'Pump', so he raised and lowered the pump handle while she rinsed the blood and dirt from the cloth.

After she had his hands and face cleaned as well as possible, she carefully brushed all the dirt she could from his clothing. She took a step back and looked him over appraisingly. 'That's the best I can do,' she announced.

'Thanks,' Ian offered, his own voice sounding lame as he said it.

'You might brush your hair down some before you come on into school,' she suggested.

She turned then and walked quickly around the corner of the building. He took a deep, ragged breath. He used his hands to smooth his hair down as much as possible. Looking around, he spotted his books, still held firmly by the leather strap, lying beside him. He didn't remember having them when Coralee led him to the pump. She must have picked them up and brought them along.

He shrugged and walked around the corner of the school building and headed for the front door. Miss Hodges was just starting to shut the door as he came up the steps.

'Mr Hennessy!' she confronted him. 'Have you been fighting?'

'Uh, no, ma'am,' he lied. 'I, uh, fell down.'

'There seems to have been an epidemic of that this morning! You look like you fell down multiple times, young man,' she declared.

'Uh, there was a bunch o' rocks there,' he mumbled as he ducked past her. He hurried to his desk and sat down, trying his best to ignore the buzz of whispers his arrival had spawned.

He darted a sideways look at Shaunnessy, who sat a couple desks over in the same row. He hadn't managed to do nearly as good a job of removing the blood and dirt from his face as Coralee had from Ian's, he guessed. In fact, he thought the bigger boy must look considerably worse than he did.

He didn't even mind Miss Hodges' pointed lecture on the evils of fighting, and her dire warning of what would ensue if she saw even a hint of any fighting on the school grounds.

4

Once again, Ian dawdled a few minutes after the teacher dismissed the class. As he had done the day before, he left the school walking directly to where he could normally expect the quartet of his oppressors to be waiting for him.

He was surprised as Coralee Hickson fell in beside him. 'Want me to walk with you?' she asked in a very matter-of-fact voice.

He stopped and turned to her. Conflicting emotions tumbled over each other in his mind, causing him to stammer.

'I, uh, no! Yes! I mean, yeah, I'd love to have you walk with me, but you'd best not today.'

'You're not going to try to fight them again are you?'

'Yup.'

'Why?'

'Cuz I'm tired o' runnin' from 'em.'

'You don't have to deliberately provoke them to keep from running from them.'

His voice was hesitant at first, but gathered steam as he talked. 'Well, I, I mean, well, yes, I do. I've run too long. Now they know I'm scared of 'em, and they know any one of 'em can whip me, so the only way I can stop 'em is to make it hurt them too much to keep doin' it. If I go right at 'em, they'll know I ain't scared no more. If I can hurt 'em enough, some of 'em at least will start bein' a-scared o' me, 'stead o' me bein' scared o' them all the time.'

Her response stunned him. 'I know where there's a big stick. I'll get it, and I'll watch from where they won't see me. If they start to kick you and things after you're already on the ground, I'll go after them with the stick. They won't hit me, because I'm a girl.'

He stared at her in disbelief. 'I don't want no girl fightin' my fights for me,' he asserted.

'I'm not going to fight your fights for you,' she argued. 'You can just go get yourself beat up all you please. But when you do, I'll keep them from killing you. That's all. Or maybe I'll just let you go and get yourself killed and see if I even care.'

Before he could answer, she walked swiftly away, the tilt of her head and swing of her hips betraying her frustration and anger.

He scratched the back of his head in confusion, then instantly regretted doing so. How did the back of his head get so sore? He took a deep breath and headed for what he was sure would be another beating.

As he approached the spot he knew they would be waiting, the quartet turned and watched him approach. Adrenaline began to surge within him. The sense of freedom from fear returned, wiping away the hard edge of pain in all the places he hurt. His steps lengthened. His speed increased.

The four who awaited him perceived

the change instantly. Glen was the first to break. 'I gotta go, you guys,' he said, as he hurried away.

'Me too,' Milton agreed. 'My pa told me not to be late tonight.'

'I gotta go too,' Stan quickly asserted, as he fell in with the fleeing pair.

Suddenly, Shaunnessy was left alone, blocking Ian's path. Ian neither slowed nor swerved. When he was three or four paces away, Shaunnessy held his hands up, palms toward Ian. He said, 'Are you nuts?'

'Ain't nuts, and I ain't afraid o' nuts,' Ian shot back.

'You know I'll just beat you up again if you don't back off.'

'So beat me up again. It'll cost you some.'

'It'll cost you more!'

'We'll see.'

Shaunnessy frowned in honest confusion. 'What for do you wanta get beat up?'

'I don't. But I ain't runnin' from you or nobody else. Not no more. Either you gotta promise to leave me alone, or you gotta beat me up every time I get close to you. Every time I get where I can reach you, I'm gonna lay into you just as hard and fast as I can. And I don't care what you do to me for it, you can't stop me.'

'I can kill you.'

'Most likely you can. For sure that's what you're gonna have to do. Then they'll hang you for it, an' we'll both be dead.'

For the first time in his life, Shaunnessy felt the sharp stab of fear. This kid half his size had made him hurt more than anyone ever had, and he wouldn't quit. He just wouldn't quit! He felt himself on the verge of tears of frustration. 'So what do ya want?'

'I want your promise to leave me alone from now on.'

'And if I don't?'

'Then I'll do my best to beat you to a pulp every time I get close to you.'

'Even if I kill you?'

'Even if you kill me. Until you kill me.'

'You're crazy!'

'And you're a coward. You only wanta hurt kids that're scared of you. Well I ain't scared of you no more. So you gonna fight me, or you gonna stand there spoutin' off hot air?'

Shaunnessy stared at this suddenly strange and unfathomable foe in utter disbelief. Finally he said, 'I don't wanta fight you.'

'Then go home an' leave me alone.'

Shaunnessy opened his mouth twice to speak, and shut it each time. Finally he whirled on his heel and stalked away.

Relief flooding through him so intensely it made his knees feel weak, Ian stood where he was and watched his greatest fear in the world walk away.

Almost at once Coralee was at his side. 'That was fantastic!' she exulted, as if the victory were hers. 'You are the bravest person I have ever known.'

Instantly self-conscious, her face turned flaming red. She wheeled and ran away, slowing to a walk only after she was a goodly distance from him.

Ian watched her flee, his brow furrowed in total confusion. A chuckle behind him brought him around in a crouch, ready to fight again. Everett Stinson stood there grinning. 'Don't try to understand the fairer sex,' he admonished. 'You never will.'

Ian turned and looked back at Coralee, already nearly out of sight, then back at the shopkeeper who had suddenly become his friend and mentor. 'Why'd Corky go an' run off like that? I didn't say nothin' wrong.'

'Don't worry about it,' Everett evaded. 'You handled yourself mighty well, though. I take it you must have had a little session with your friends before school today.'

Ian grinned. 'Yeah. I mean, yessir. I, uh, I thought about it some last night. I know what way all of 'em come to school, and where they most gen'rly meet up. I sorta thought if I caught each one of 'em afore they got together,

I could deal with 'em one at a time.'

'You must have found them.'

'Yessir. It worked real good. I can whip 'em, one at a time. 'Cept for Shaunnessy. He beat me up again, but I managed to hurt 'im real good whilst he was a-doin' it. So tonight he up an' promised he wouldn't pick on me no more, if I'd stop tyin' into 'im every time I see 'im.'

'And how did Miss Hickson get involved in all this?'

'She seen Shaunnessy beat me up this mornin'. She went an' got all the blood an' dirt cleaned off'n me afore I went in to school. At the pump out back. She had a rag or somethin' with her.'

'A handkerchief.'

'Yeah. Somethin' like that.'

'So you went into school looking better than any of the other four?'

'Yeah, I 'spect so, 'cause of Corky. Must've anyhow, 'cause the other kids was doin' a lot o' pointin' at them guys an' whisperin', then lookin' back at me.'

'What'll you bet that the rumors will be all over town by tomorrow that you whipped all four of them all by yourself?'

'But I didn't. I got plumb beat up.'

'But you beat them.'

'How'd I beat 'em, if they beat me up?'

'You forced them to take everything you could dish out in order to beat you up. You stopped running. You made it cost them dearly to bully you. So they became afraid of you, instead of you being afraid of them. Even though they can beat you up if they decide to, they won't, because they're afraid of you now.'

Ian thought about it a long moment. 'That feels good,' he said finally. 'Havin' someone else a-scared o' me, I mean.'

'Don't let that become a problem, now,' Everett admonished.

Ian frowned. 'What d'ya mean?'

'There is a very real danger,' the merchant lectured, 'that now that you have established your prowess and

48

fearlessness, that you might be tempted to become the bully, and try to enforce your wishes on others against their will.'

'Oh, I wouldn't never do that.'

'Listen! Remember what I'm telling you. You are probably the best natural-born fighter that I have ever seen. In a few years, it's doubtful if any man will be able to stand before you empty-handed. Then you will realize that you have the ability to intimidate others, and to strike fear into the hearts of brave men. In the excitement of a moment, when you know you are able to force others to bend to your will, you will be tempted to do so.'

'I don't think so, Mr Stinson.'

'Just keep it in mind, for the time that temptation comes,' he repeated. 'You must never become the bully. Especially in your relationships with the fairer sex. You must never, ever use your strength or your will to try to force anyone to do something they do not wish to do.'

Confusion rambled around the corners of Ian's mind as he tried to grasp what the merchant obviously felt was a very important lesson. Finally he just mumbled, 'Yessir.'

'You'd best head for home now,' the storekeeper suggested.

He hadn't made it all the way home when Clancy O'Toole suddenly blocked his path. The big Irishman was the older, even bigger version of his son. He towered over Ian, hands on his hips. 'Be you the dirty whelp what tooken a club to me son?' he demanded.

'I didn't take no club to 'im,' Ian protested. 'He beat me up, is what he did, but I got in a few good licks.'

' 'Tis seein' what you did to him that I did,' the elder O'Toole raged. 'No sawed-off little runt like you could ever be puttin' a mark on me Shaunnessy, and he's been just plain beat up! 'Tis a club you must've used, and now I'm gonna be whippin' the livin' daylights outa you for it.'

Stark fear drained the blood from

Ian's face. Aside from the difference in size and strength, it would be unthinkable for him to defy the authority of an adult to try to fight the man. The anger in the big man's face made him literally fear for his life.

As Clancy reached out for him, Ian felt himself brushed aside. Everett Stinson stood where he had been a second before. O'Toole was instantly taken aback. Everett spoke first. 'I saw the fight, Clancy. You're right that it wasn't a fair fight. Your son and three of his friends ganged up on the Hennessy boy, here. He did an admirable job of holding his own against four much larger boys who are all too cowardly to try to face him one on one.'

O'Toole's face instantly turned purple with rage. 'Are you callin' me boy a coward?'

'Yes. That's exactly what I'm calling him,' Everett asserted in a calm voice. 'I assume it's a trait he has learned from the poor excuse of a father he is burdened with, judging from your

51

willingness to assault a thirteen-year-old boy.'

O'Toole fairly sputtered with rage. 'This ain't for bein' none o' your business, Stinson, so get yourself lost somewhere.'

'This is my business,' Everett disputed. 'I have made it my business.'

'Then 'tis you I'll be beatin' instead o' him!'

'You can certainly try,' Everett agreed. 'But I believe I'm a little old to be engaged in brawling with idiots. If you make any move to assault me, I will put a bullet right between your eyes.'

The eyes the merchant mentioned bulged with surprise and rage. ' 'Tis not even a gun you're havin'.'

From some place neither Ian nor Clancy saw, a gun appeared in Everett's hand. The barrel was less than four inches from the bridge of the elder O'Toole's nose. The Irishman's eyes widened even further, and crossed as both eyes tried to focus on the unexpected weapon.

Clancy took a quick step backward. He glanced around as if seeking witnesses to some affront or crime. As his eyes returned, the shopkeeper stood before him, empty hands hanging at his sides. There was no gun in sight.

O'Toole was at a total loss for words, and had even less idea of what to do next. The burden of needing to do anything was relieved by the bewildering merchant. 'I will tell you this one time, Clancy,' he said. His voice was quiet, but there was no mistaking the hard edge of steel in it. 'I have shot rabid dogs for whom I had more respect than I have for you. It would not cause me a moment's concern or a minute's loss of sleep to send you to hell where you belong. So listen very closely to what I am about to tell you. I do not want you, I do not want your son, I do not want any of your son's friends, to bother this young man in any way whatsoever, now or at any time in the future. If you do, or if they do, you will answer to me. If that were to happen, be assured I will find you, I will find you quickly, and I will instantly and permanently rid this world of your unsavory presence. Do you understand me, Mr O'Toole?'

Eyes bugging in disbelief, Clancy looked the merchant up and down, clearly seeking something to offer assurance that the storekeeper could not, or would not, make good on his threat. Instead he saw a quiet and steely resolve that left no trace of doubt that the man meant every word he had said. Remembering the incredible appearance and subsequent disappearance of the Navy Colt down whose barrel he had so recently stared, he experienced a level of fear he had never known.

'Just make sure the kid leaves me boy alone,' he blustered, as he scurried away.

Ian stared in open-mouthed amazement at the merchant. Neither the man's face nor his voice offered any hint of stress as he said, 'I suspect your mother is waiting for you, Ian.'

'Uh, yessir.'

He looked toward home for a long moment. He thought he should at least thank the man. He turned back to frame the words to do so. The storekeeper was nowhere to be seen.

5

'Naw, I just gotta get outa here.'

Everett Stinson eyed the young man standing before him. He ran a hand through the gray hair above his left temple. 'Well, I suppose,' he agreed, reluctance dragging back against his words like a loaded stone boat.

Ian looked again at the fresh mound of dirt beside which the two remained standing. The others had left. What few mourners there were had gone to the church for the ubiquitous 'funeral lunch'. The grave diggers had finished their work. There was no longer any reason for them to stay.

'I don't suppose she left you much of anything,' Everett probed.

Ian shook his head. He swiped at a rebellious tear that insisted on sliding down his cheek. 'Naw,' he said again. 'Ma didn't have nothin' to leave. Even afore the consumption took hold of her, it was all she could do to feed her'n me.'

'Well, you were a big help to her.'

Ian shrugged. 'I done what I could. She wouldn't let me quit school. I could've worked more if she had.'

'Well, you've been a good hand for me, even so,' Everett assured him. 'The job at the store is still yours, if you want to keep it.'

'Naw,' Ian said yet again. 'I'm obliged an' all, but I think maybe as how I'll head out West a ways.'

Everett eyed him carefully. 'It's a different world out there.'

'I 'spect. Can't be worse than this one. Might be a whole lot better. I'd sorta like to learn how to be a cowboy. Maybe get myself a ranch some day.'

Everett stared off into the distance. 'I used to think that's what I wanted to do. Be part of the settling of the West. Not to ranch, though. I thought of setting up a gunsmith shop somewhere that was just starting to get settled.

Grow with the land.'

'So how come you didn't?'

Everett took a deep breath. 'Well, I got married, is the biggest reason. My wife didn't have any desire to leave Iowa. I talked her into coming here to Sioux City, because it's at least clear over here on the western edge of Iowa. I either had to put roots down here or live out West alone. Once I met Irma, I didn't want to be alone anymore. It's a lonely place out there, by yourself.'

'You didn't never have no kids,' Ian observed.

Another deep sigh escaped the emotional lock the older man maintained. 'No, we never did,' he said. 'We tried. We wanted a family. She was actually with child once, but lost it early, and nearly died. The doctor said she would never be able to have children. I guess he was right.'

Ian supposed he ought to say something next, but he had no idea what to say. At sixteen he didn't have a wealth of experience from which to draw an appropriate word of consolation.

It was Everett who broke the awkward silence. 'At least you've got the house.'

Ian nodded. 'I'll be sellin' it, I 'spect. It oughta sell for enough to give me a stake, at least.'

'It's a well-built house,' Everett agreed. 'Your pa built it to last. He planned on coming back after the war and filling it with family.'

That stubbornly rebellious tear fought its way down Ian's face again. He swiped at it with more than slight irritation. 'You know anyone that'd wanta buy it?'

Everett thought it over for a while. 'Let me do some figuring on it,' he said. 'You're going to need a good horse, a saddle and bridle, a bedroll, some staples for food and something to cook them in. A coffee pot you can use on a campfire. A Dutch oven and a frying pan. You'll sure need a good rifle and pistol, a decent supply of ammunition for both, and enough money to live on until you find something.'

Ian turned the list over in his mind. 'More'n I'd thought about,' he admitted.

They walked together back to the church where Ian endured all the offers of sympathy he could stand. When he had a chance he slipped outside and headed for home.

Two days later he stood with Everett at the area Everett test-fired the guns he repaired as part of his business. Everett wore a gunbelt Ian had never seen the shopkeeper wear before.

'I ain't never seen you wear that,' Ian quizzed.

Everett shrugged. 'I wear it often enough to keep my hand in shape, but I never make a show of it. I don't suppose most folks even know I own it.'

'I sure didn't, an' I been workin' for you a couple years a'ready.'

Instead of answering, Everett handed a holstered pistol, its cartridge belt wrapped around it, to Ian. 'Here. Try this on for size.'

Ian's eyes opened wide. He looked back and forth from the gun to the merchant several times, then took it. As he had worked at learning both the hardware and gunsmith trades, he had fantasized about owning a gun and holster of his own. The one Stinson handed him was far more expensive than he had dreamed of owning.

He belted it around his waist and tied the leather throng around his thigh. 'Not so tight,' Everett corrected. 'If you tie it that tight, it'll wear and gall when you move. You want it tight enough the holster doesn't move when you draw, but not tight enough to bother you.'

Ian loosened and retied the thong, watching his mentor for approval when he had it right. When he was finished, Everett said, 'Now I want you to watch. Do you see those tin cans out there?' He pointed to a row of half a dozen cans.

Ian nodded, then he nearly jumped out of his skin as the gun in Everett's hand barked. One of the cans flew into the air, then bounced along the ground before coming to rest. Before it stopped bouncing, the gun was back in the storekeeper's holster.

Mouth agape, Ian stared. 'How'd you do that?' he demanded.

'Slowly, to be perfectly honest.'

'Slow! I didn't even see you move.'

'Well, watch again, then.'

In a blur of speed the pistol seemed to fairly leap into the man's hand, barking at the same moment the barrel came up. The already punctured can once again flew into the air.

'Wow!' Ian breathed. 'You gotta be the fastest man with a gun what ever was!'

'Not even close. I'm slow,' Everett disputed. 'I'm old and slow. If you're going to wear a gun, you're going to have to make a decision how you wear it. If you wear it up high on your belt, either butt backward on the right side or butt forward on the other side, so you can draw across your body, you're announcing that it's just a tool of a cowboy's trade. But if you're going to wear it as a weapon, then you need to learn how to use it well. You learn fast, and you're about the quickest person with your hands that I've ever seen. If you want to learn, I'll teach you.'

'You mean you can teach me to do that? Like you just done, I mean?'

Everett nodded, his face far more solemn than Ian could remember. 'Against that inner voice that chides me for doing so, yes,' he said. 'I will teach you, if you make me two promises.'

'What two promises?'

'One, that you will become as good as you possibly can. As with all things, it is not enough for you to just *do* something. You must do it as well as you can possibly do it. If you are capable of doing it better than anyone else, then you must do it better than anyone else. Never, ever settle for being mediocre.'

'You think I can be that good with a gun?'

'I am quite sure you can, if you live long enough.'

'What's the second promise?'

'That you will never, ever, use a gun on anybody except as an absolute last resort. It is the same with a gun as I taught you to be with fighting. Never, ever, run away from a fight. But never, ever be the one who starts it. If you have to fight, then fight to win, any way you can, just as fast as you can. If you're not going to do that, then settle for being a coward and run away.'

'I ain't never gonna run away from nobody or nothin' for the whole rest o' my life,' Ian vowed.

As if he had said nothing, the older man continued, 'Part of that is deciding here and now that you will never draw your gun against anybody you are not going to shoot. There must never be even an instant's hesitation between drawing and shooting. It must be one motion, one act. More men die when they draw their gun because they hesitate an instant to be sure they want to go ahead and shoot. By the time they decide to do so, they're the one who's been shot.'

A tight knot formed suddenly in Ian's gut. This was life and death his mentor was talking about. He was offering to teach him something that might cost him his life. On the other hand, he had heard enough to know that a cowboy's life was rough and tumble at best. He was too small to hold his own in a brawl, even though he had found he could give an awfully good accounting of himself. If he was to be taken seriously in that mysterious and exciting land known as 'out West', he guessed he had better learn to use the gun.

Everett stood patiently, watching the conflicting emotions play across the youngster's face. It was several minutes before Ian finally took a deep breath and said, 'OK. I promise.'

'It'll also mean you'll have to postpone your plans to head out West,' Everett cautioned. 'The things you need to learn can't be taught in a week or two.'

Ian thought it over for a long moment. 'Makes sense to be ready afore I head out,' he concluded.

For the next two weeks, Ian's arm ached day and night. His hand blistered and the blisters broke. By the third week the blisters began to give way to calluses and the weight of the gun became less burdensome. It wasn't until the sixth week, practicing under the watchful eye of the master gunsmith, that he could both draw somewhat quickly and shoot more or less accurately.

During that time he carried out his duties at the store, did a semblance of housekeeping, learned to ride the horse that Everett recommended he buy, and familiarized himself with all the gear and tack his tutor told him he must learn to use. Week after week, his proficiency with both gun and gear grew steadily.

The wisdom and knowledge of the merchant never ceased to amaze him.

At the end of four months he felt as if he had learned a lifetime of knowledge, skill and lore. What he didn't know was that he had scarce begun to learn.

He was also learning, against his will, how much he did not want to move away and leave Coralee Hickson. During the last couple of years of school and since, he had spent more and more time with her. Her family had him over for supper often, and treated him as part of the family.

She was dumbstruck by his intention to leave, at first. Then she was angry and resentful. Then she grew resigned to the idea. Before he left, they pledged to write to each other. As soon as he found a job, he would write to her and tell her where to send letters to him. They promised to wait for each other.

The taste of her lips, when she gave him that lingering good-bye kiss, stayed with him for days, and its memory stayed always fresh in his mind. Someday, he promised himself, he'd be back for Corky Hickson.

6

He led the dapple gray gelding down the ramp from the train car in which it had traveled. Its ears were laid back, its eyes rolling back and forth. If not for the firm hand on the bridle, he might have bolted at the strange sights, sounds and smells.

Ian Hennessy understood perfectly how his horse felt. He, too, felt as if he had been picked up, carried off somewhere, and set down in a strange and different world. Chugwater, the conductor had said it was called. Ridiculous name for a town, he had said. The name came from the sound the buffalo made when the Indians chased them off the big cliff. Chug, he had said, over and over in a deep voice, Chug, Chug, Chug. At the west end, the conductor had told him, there's a chunk of cliff that isn't connected to the other one called Chimney Rock, and a valley where ranchers had wintered cattle for many years. Almost the end of the railroad; not a place anyone with a brain would be getting off the train. If for no other reason, Ian would have gotten off the train there just so he wouldn't have to listen to anything else the conductor said.

A cluster of corrals made of rough-cut planks and crooked posts flanked the railroad track. From the corrals, two separate chutes ramped up to the level of the floor of stock cars, enabling livestock to be loaded for transport. No animals were in the corrals, but the well-trampled ground within attested to their recent presence.

Ian took a deep breath and looked toward town. It looked to him more like a ramshackle collection of thrown-together buildings, shacks and lean-to structures than a town. At the far end, about a hundred yards from the end of the town itself, a cluster of tepees hugged the side of the road.

The streets of the town were crooked, with no sharp line to indicate where they started or stopped. Even the signs of the businesses were mostly roughly painted announcements of the nature of the business than anything that seemed business-like or professional.

In the distance beyond the excuse of a town a strange bluff rose from the almost barren ground. It towered nearly sixty feet in the air, rising in a steep cliff that appeared to be the edge of some huge mesa. In his mind, he could see the huge buffalo toppling over its edge, crashing to the ground below. 'Chug,' the conductor's voice in his head repeated. At the western end of the cliff there was a lower space, then a single butte that rose to the same height. 'Chimney Rock,' that same voice in his head said.

The other direction held as vast a panorama of nothing as he had ever seen. Scrub sage, bunch grass and soap weeds were interspersed with patches of buffalo grass. The bunch grass was tall, but looked coarse and uninviting. The buffalo grass was no taller than two or three inches at its tallest. It all looked scraggly and twisted, as if it were wrung all out of shape by the winds that swept across the empty land. Hills and small valleys seemed to be interrupted by frequent gullies. Some were shallow and narrow. Others appeared deep enough to have trees growing in the bottoms, whose uppermost branches failed to reach above the rolling hills. In some he could see various kinds of bushes struggling for a foothold in the rocky soil.

Far off to the west and north the country rose to greater heights, backed by purplish-blue mountains. Only the bottom portions of those mountains were visible. The rest were mostly a pure white that reflected back the sun with painful brilliance. It took him a while to realize they were almost entirely covered with snow, even now in early spring.

The wind blowing off those snow fields sent chills shuddering through him despite the awkward-feeling fur-lined vest Everett had assured him would be standard wear out here.

He walked, leading his horse, down the town's street until he saw a sign indicating a livery barn. He stopped uncertainly at the door. He was almost ready to turn back around and leave when a voice said, 'Mornin'.'

He blinked into the dimness of the interior, making out the form of a man limping toward him. 'Need your horse put up?'

'Uh, yes. Uh, do I leave the saddle and stuff with him, or do I take it with me?'

The hostler looked him over, eyes dancing. 'Fresh off'n the train from New Yawk City, are ya?'

'Uh, no. Uh, Sioux City, Iowa, actually.'

'Jist as well be New Yawk,' the hostler asserted. 'What in Sam Hill you doin' in this country?'

'I, uh, want to be a cowboy.'

The hostler snorted. 'That ain't as easy as folks think,' he said. 'Where'd ya go gettin' a lame-brained idea like that?'

Ian flushed, suddenly tired of being the object of such obvious derision. 'Oh, it just sort of came to me the same day the wind blew off a big tree branch that hit me in the head,' he said.

Unexpectedly the hostler tipped back his head and cackled. 'Now that's a good one, that is.'

He looked Ian, the horse, and the visible gear over carefully. 'Well, somebody outfitted ya who knowed what he was doin', at least,' he approved.

Ian nodded. 'He taught me what he could, I guess. It feels pretty strange, though.'

'Yeah, well, you look like you feel purty strange,' the old man agreed. 'But at least you don't come along pretendin' to know a lot you don't. If you get on with the right outfit, keep your eyes an' ears open, an' work your butt off, you just might make it.'

'So what's the right outfit?'

The hostler's eyebrows shot up. He pursed his lips. He looked Ian over again. 'Well, I'll tell you what. Amos Plover's in town. Likely over at the Silver Dollar. He runs the Two-Bar. He's been known to take on a green hand now an' again. Tell 'im Harvey sent ya.'

'Two-Bar? What's a Two-Bar?'

'The Two-Bar's a cattle ranch, over toward the mountains. Their brand's just two bars. No letters or numbers. Just two bars.' He bent down and scratched the brand in the dirt. 'Like that. So it's just called the Two-Bar.'

Ian started to leave, then turned back. 'You didn't tell me what to do with my stuff.'

'Take your bedroll an' your saddle-bags with ya. Go over to the hotel down the street there an' rent yourself a room. Leave your stuff in the room an' go on over to the saloon. Your stuff'll be all right in your room.'

'I don't need to take my saddle?'

'Nope. I'll take care o' that, an' take care o' your horse. Fifty cents a day.'

'OK. Do I pay you now?'

'Pay when you leave.'

'OK. Thanks.'

He secured his bedroll and saddlebags, hoisted them along with the large, fully packed carpet valise that held the rest of his belongings and headed for the door.

'Oh, kid?'

He stopped and turned partially around. 'Yeah?'

'Good luck.'

'Thanks.'

He followed the old hostler's advice, secured the room and piled his stuff on the floor. He mulled the idea of whether to strap on a gun, and decided against it. He had already decided that, at least for the time being, he would wear one of the two pistols he now owned high on his belt on the left side, butt forward, because it seemed the easiest access when he was mounted.

The knife Everett insisted he also carry rode in its sheath just behind the pistol. He knew from his mentor's endless lectures that both the gun and knife were essential parts of a cowboy's gear when he was working.

He didn't know if, in time, he would wear the other pistol on his right hip, low and tied down, for a quick draw. If he did, he hadn't decided whether he'd still wear the other one too, or just wear one at a time. For the time being, he opted to wear neither. That felt more natural for him anyway.

As he crossed the dusty street, he caught a movement from the corner of his eye. He jerked his head around just in time to see a man disappear into a store. Something about him seemed vaguely familiar, but he couldn't say why. He frowned briefly, then shrugged his shoulders. Wouldn't be anyone I know clear out here, he assured himself.

When he walked into the Silver Dollar Saloon he instantly learned what 'center of attention' meant. Abrupt silence spread through the place. Every eye was riveted on him. Several grinned openly. A couple noticeably frowned. Most just stared.

His own voice sounding unnaturally loud in the deathly silence, he said, 'Uh, is Amos Plover here?'

Half a dozen heads turned. From the direction of their stare, Ian picked out the man he sought instantly.

Amos sat with his back to the wall at one of the round tables. A hat that was easily as big as the one that felt so unwieldy on Ian's head was pushed to the back of Plover's head. In contrast to the bright, clean newness of Ian's, the hat was stained dark for two inches above the sweatband, and showed a good deal of wear. His oversized moustache drooped down past his mouth on both sides, giving him a dour expression. A match jutting from the corner of his mouth abruptly changed ends of his mouth. 'I guess I'm here,' he said. 'What can I do for you?'

'Uh, Harvey told me you might be hiring. I'm looking for a job.'

Three people out of Ian's range of vision chuckled audibly. Several others grinned. 'You a cowboy, are you?' Amos asked, his face as serious as that of a judge.

Ian grinned in spite of his nervousness. 'Oh, no, sir,' he said quickly. 'I ain't never done nothin' like that. Not yet. But I work hard, and learn real quick.'

Amos opened his mouth to reply, then closed it again. Silently he watched a man in his mid to upper-thirties saunter up to Ian. His oversize belly hung far enough over his belt it was impossible to tell whether he wore one. His shirt was half unbuttoned, hairy chest and broad shoulders belying the soft appearance of his gut. His stringy hair fell to his shoulders. A brown streak of tobacco juice traced a thin line downward from the corner of his mouth.

He stood in front of Ian, slowly

looking him up and down. Finally he said, 'My, my! Ain't this here somethin', boys? Just lookee this outfit this fella's sportin'! Don't he look just like somethin' outa one o' them there dime novels?'

A couple chuckles greeted his words, and it was adequate to fuel his desire to use Ian as the evening's sport.

He rolled the cud of tobacco in his mouth from one cheek to the other, then said, 'You know, boys, this here outfit's just too dad-gummed fine to fit in around here. Why them boots ain't even got a speck o' nothin' on 'em. Here. I'll take care o' fixin' that, at least.'

He instantly spat a brown streak of tobacco juice that included a generous amount of the tobacco itself directly on to one of Ian's boots. Again, two or three chuckles greeted the action.

Ian didn't even think about what he was doing. For the barest instant he was aghast that anyone would do such a thing without provocation. Then anger surged up wildly within him. Without thought, his right fist shot forward. By the time it reached the other man's chin, it carried his weight and strength behind it, as well as the stress and tension that had tied his stomach into knots. It landed with a 'thunk' that sounded throughout the saloon. The man's head snapped back. His feet lifted momentarily clear of the floor. He sprawled backward, sawdust spraying outward. He lay without moving.

A collective gasp from a dozen mouths broke the dam of silence, and were followed instantly by as many excited voices.

'Wow!'

'Did you see that?'

'That little runt knocked Tub flat on his back!'

'Cold-cocked him, that's what he did.'

'Tub never even saw that one comin'.'

'Who is that greenhorn?'

'He still ain't got that purty new outfit dirty.'

''Ceptin' one o' the boots.'

That last comment prompted Ian to look down at the boots that had seen almost no wear. The big brown splotch on the top of the left one sent anger surging back through him again. He stepped over to the prone figure on the floor and wiped the top of his boot clean along the prone man's pant leg.

He turned back to Amos. 'I'm sorry about that, Mr Plover. I, uh, I didn't really mean to do that. He shouldn'ta spit on my new boots, though.'

Amos grinned. 'I'm guessin' it'll be a day or two before he tries that on anyone else, too. You throw a mighty fine punch for your size.'

Unsure how to respond, Ian said, 'I really do need a job, sir.'

'Can you ride a horse?'

'Yessir. I got my own horse. He's over at the livery barn.'

'Got all your gear?'

Ian hesitated a long moment. 'Well, I think so, yeah. Anyway it's everythin' Mr Stinson — he's a friend o' mine that's been tryin' to teach me — I got everythin' he thought I needed.'

'You got folks?'

'No, sir.'

'No kin?'

'No, sir. My pa, he got kilt in the war. Ma, she died o' the consumption a few months ago.'

'So you decided to come out West and be a cowboy.'

'Yessir. If it works out, an' I learn an' all that, I thought maybe I could get me a ranch o' my own some day.'

Amos studied the earnest gaze of the youngster's dark eyes for a long while. 'Well, I'll give you the chance. Be at the livery barn at sunup tomorrow, ready to ride.'

Ian grinned from ear to ear. 'Thank you, sir. I'll be there. You can bet on it.'

He wheeled and almost ran out the door, eager to escape before the rancher changed his mind.

He stopped off at the post office, the sign of which he had noted on the way to the Silver Dollar. Standing at the tall desk, he spent nearly an hour writing a letter to Corky. He described the train ride, the town, the country around it, the mountains in the distance, the address to which she could send him letters, and even his confrontation in the saloon. When he had written everything he could think of to tell her, he hesitated a long time. Then he wrote, 'Affectionately yours,' and signed his name. He hoped that wasn't too forward of him.

The first rays of the sun found him, horse saddled, valise tied on to the top of his bedroll, waiting.

Amos Plover nodded approvingly. He carefully looked over Ian's horse and gear.

'You got a slicker?' he asked.

'A what?'

'A slicker. A raincoat.'

'Why do I need a raincoat?'

Amos sighed and grinned. 'Boy, you are green, ain't ya? A slicker is a raincoat that's made for wearin' on a horse. It's got an extra cape across the shoulders to get the water to run off'n you, an' it's split up a ways from the bottom, so it'll spread out an' cover your legs on both sides o' your horse.'

'But why do I need one?'

Amos sighed again, almost grinning around the ubiquitous match that constantly moved from one corner of his mouth to the other. 'Out here, son, the first thing you gotta do to stay alive is stay wet on the inside an' dry on the outside. If you dry out inside — meanin' if you ain't smart enough to carry along water or know where to find some, an' keep drinkin' reg'lar — you'll either dry out in the sun an' die in the summer, or dry out an' freeze from the inside out in the winter. But if you get wet on the outside, you'll feel OK in the summer till the sun goes down, but once the sun drops off behind them mountains yonder, she gets plumb chilly in a hurry. If'n you're wet, an' your clothes is wet, you'll be shiverin' like a stray pup surrounded by a pack o' coyotes in half an hour, an' you'll get cold enough to die from it in a couple or three hours.'

Ian frowned, digesting the information, so Amos repeated himself. 'So make sure you stay wet on the inside an' dry on the outside.'

'It sounds like it's sort of a chore just staying alive out here.'

Amos nodded. 'It is for a fact. Ten times as many men die from bein' too cold or too hot or from flash floods or lightnin' or blizzards or mad cows or scared horses or rattlesnakes or a dozen other things, than what gets kilt by somebody.'

For whatever reason, Ian's mind picked up on *mad cows*. 'Mad cows?' he echoed. 'Aren't mad bulls more dangerous?'

Amos shook his head. 'Naw. Bulls don't generally bother ya none. Not unless you're pushin' 'em, or tryin' to keep 'em from fightin' when a bunch of 'em are together. But cows get mad for pertnear any reason, or no reason at all.

Especially when they got a calf. An' a bull, if'n he does get mad, will put his head down an' come a chargin' at ya. Your horse won't even get excited about that. He'll just step outa the way an' let 'im charge on by. But if a cow's mad at ya, she'll come in with her head up an' her eyes wide open, and she'll be plumb hard to git away from. Most cowpokes would a whole lot rather face a rattler with nothin' but a rock or two in his hand than have to deal with a mad cow.'

When the lad didn't reply, Amos said, 'Well, let's stop by Gunnard's Mercantile and pick you up a slicker, and then we'll head out to the ranch. You got money to buy one?'

'Yessir.'

'Then tie your horse on behind and climb up here in the buckboard with me. I'll wear your ears out all the way out to the ranch with more stuff than you'll ever remember, and we'll find out what you're made of. The ranch is better'n twenty miles toward them mountains. We'll be all day and half the night gettin' there.'

Once more, Ian didn't respond, lost in wondering if he were capable of learning enough, fast enough, to stay alive long enough to even start being a cowboy. He was jarred from his reverie by a glimpse of someone watching him from the corner of a building. He turned his head around for a better look, but whoever it was had already jerked back out of sight. He frowned.

'Somethin' wrong?' the rancher asked.

He shook his head. 'No. Not really. That's just the second time I got a real quick glimpse o' somebody that seemed sorta familiar, somehow.'

The rancher chuckled. 'That'll get worse, the older ya git,' he assured the youngster. 'By the time you're my age everybody ya see'll remind ya of someone you knowed some time or other.'

Ian supposed that was probably true.

Still, there was something vaguely unsettling about that glimpse, and the way whoever it was seemed to duck out of sight quickly whenever he turned that way.

7

'Are you sure that's a ridin' horse?'

The grizzled face of the foreman showed no expression, though his eyes were dancing. 'Well, he ain't just now, but he's got the makings of a right good horse. All he needs is for you to break 'im to suit yourself. Make 'im your horse.'

The horse in question looked like anything in the world except something that would ever allow himself to be ridden. True, it was Ian's saddle that graced his back. It was a hackamore, rather than Ian's bridle on his head, however. Chet Hunley, the Two-Bar foreman, had a firm grip on that hackamore. Great muscles bulged in his arm and shoulder, and it was obviously all he could do to maintain control of the animal.

The horse's ears were laid back flat

against his head. His eyes, wide and bulging, rolled wildly, jumping from Ian to the cowboy holding him to the row of grinning ranch hands that lined the top rail of the corral. His nostrils flared. His feet were widely planted as he leaned back against the restraining hand with all his strength. Every breath rasping through his bared teeth sounded like something halfway between a wheeze and a growl.

'He looks like a wild animal!' Ian breathed.

'Well, now, I guess he is, sorta,' the foreman admitted. 'They all start out thataway, you know. Once he finds out you're the boss, an' that you ain't gonna hurt 'im, he'll settle right down.'

Ian's mind played back one of the countless conversations Everett Stinson had initiated. He remembered especially the words, 'When you hire on somewhere, the first thing they will do is put you on a raw bronc. They won't expect you to ride it, but they will expect you to try. Hang on to that saddle horn for all you're worth. And when you get bucked off, it's important that you get up and get back on again. If you can, pay attention to the horse's rhythm when he bucks. Every horse has a rhythm. If you pay attention to it, you can guess when he's going to buck the next time, and what direction he's going to go. It's not something I really know how to explain, but you'll figure out what I mean when the time comes.'

All Ian knew just then was that everything in him said this wasn't when that time ought to come. Not now. He'd only been on the Two-Bar for three days. He'd already learned more things than he thought there were to know. Now they wanted him to try to ride this wild and angry animal that obviously wanted to kill him.

He shook his head. 'I ain't sure I'm ready for that yet,' he said. His own voice sounded lame and frightened to him.

Chet frowned. 'You ain't gonna show yella, are you?'

A flood of memories washed through the young man's mind. Of all things in the world, that was the word he most feared and hated. He clamped his jaw. He pulled the oversized hat down tightly on to his head, bending the tops of his ears down in the process. He reached a hand out toward the horse, reaching for the saddle horn.

Even though he was reaching for it, he was fully four feet from able to reach it. He took a tentative step toward the horse with his left foot. His right foot refused to follow, staying firmly planted in the well-churned dirt of the round breaking corral. The effect was to place him in an awkward, spraddle-legged stance, leaning forward, straining toward the saddle horn that was still well out of reach.

He tried again, but once more it was only his left foot that co-operated, spreading his feet even more widely apart. Several of the hands on the corral fence laughed aloud.

The sound of their laughter stabbed

through him like a hot iron. It steeled his resolve and sent a surge of anger welling up within him. He straightened up and lowered the hand that was reaching for the horse. His right foot belatedly decided to join the activity in which the rest of his body was engaged. He took a deep breath and strode with determination to the struggling beast. He left foot scarcely touched the stirrup as he flung himself into the saddle. As if his often riding of a well-broken horse had taught it where to go, his right foot instantly found its stirrup.

The momentum of leaping into the saddle threw him forward onto the saddle horn, almost onto the horse's neck. Instead of immediately righting himself, he used the position to reach out and grab the hackamore reins that trailed on the ground.

He sat up straight in the saddle and grabbed hold of the saddle horn. As if that were a signal, Chet released his grip on the hackamore and stepped back.

A great shudder passed through the horse. For the barest instant Ian thought maybe he wasn't going to buck after all. He was swiftly relieved of that misconception.

The horse issued a squeal of fear and rage and exploded high into the air. Ian felt almost as if he were flying, then everything beneath him seemed to vanish and he plummeted downward. He thought for an instant he had left the saddle, but then it slammed into his backside as if permanently implanting itself there. The horse's hoofs hit the ground with a bone-jarring crash that sent pain from Ian's tail bone to the base of his skull.

He had no time to recover from the shock of that blow before the animal twisted a quarter turn and leaped into the air again, arching his back so that Ian felt as if he were perched on a giant ball that bounced sideways suddenly and once more crashed to the ground with bone-crunching force.

Only the death-grip his right hand

maintained on the saddle horn kept him from being flung off the side. Though he was still in the saddle, he was leaning to the right when the horse hit the ground, and the shock of the landing shot excruciating pain through the small of his back, up through his stomach and back, exploding out through his shoulder as if some part of his bones had been forced out through the flesh.

As the downward force of the landing changed into the upward surge of the next jump, he felt his head snap backward then forward. A red haze momentarily covered his vision.

The pain both fueled his anger and blocked out everything around him. All sound was gone except the roaring in his ears. Nothing broke the red haze of his vision except the top of the horse's head and his ears. He felt suddenly as if he were suspended in an alien place where nothing existed except himself and the horse that was trying its best to unseat him. Everything seemed to be happening in slow motion.

Somewhere in the back of his mind a deep, almost ghostly voice echoed, 'pay attention to the horse's rhythm'. Instantly it was there. He could sense, somehow, that the horse was going to spin to the left on the next jump. He leaned slightly that way, tightening his knees against the saddle's swells to brace himself. All the repeated instructions Everett had drilled into him began to make sense. Remembering them gave him a sense that he just might be capable of riding this animal.

He had remembered to turn his toes outward, hooking the rowels of his spurs in the cinch. At the top of the jump he put extra pressure on his spurs, pressed into the cinch on each side. He found it much easier to hold himself down into the saddle as the horse plummeted back toward the ground.

As soon as the upward pressure eased, he pushed down on the stirrups, shifting his weight to his feet. As the horse hit the ground, his knees absorbed most of the shock. No searing pain shot upward through his torso that time.

He found himself watching the horse's head, especially his ears. As if he could read the beast's mind through his ears, he realized he could sense the animal's intent and brace himself for it. His leaps and twists took on a definite rhythm that became easier and easier to anticipate and follow.

The red haze that had clouded his vision began to clear. The roar in his ears gave way to the cheers and yells of the ranch hands.

Abruptly the horse stopped bucking and stood, spraddle-legged, tossing his head.

'Don't let 'im stop,' Chet called out to him. 'Hit 'im with your spurs. Make him run back an' forth a few times.'

That was the last thing in the world Ian wanted to do. He wanted off of that animal. He wanted to try to work the kinks out of his back and legs and neck and arms. He wanted to try to unfasten his hand from the saddle horn where it refused to loosen its grip.

Instead he did as he was bidden. As soon as the spurs touched the horse's sides he exploded again. Ian reeled wildly in the saddle. The horse leaped forward, running as if he meant to smash himself and his rider against the far side of the corral. At the very last minute he spun to the side, once again nearly leaving Ian behind.

He had no sooner recovered his balance than the other side of the corral loomed. This time Ian instinctively hauled the reins to one side, pulling hard. The horse had no choice but to turn that way or ram the fence. He spun that direction and raced back across the corral.

As he neared the fence Ian hauled the other direction on the reins, forcing him to turn the other way. 'Thataboy!' Chet yelled. 'That's the way you show 'im who's boss!'

Half a dozen more times they sped

back and forth across the corral before the foreman yelled, 'That's prob'ly enough.'

He hauled back on the reins. The horse tossed his head once but squatted his hind legs and skidded to a halt.

'Now hang on to them reins an' get down and rub 'im down some,' Chet yelled. 'Scratch his ears an' talk to him. Love on 'im like he's your best friend. Let 'im know you ain't mad at 'im an' you ain't gonna hurt 'im.'

Obediently Ian stepped from the saddle. His right hand was still attached immovably to the saddle horn. It was fortunate that it was. His legs refused to hold him up. He would have fallen in a heap on the ground if that right hand wasn't holding him.

In a moment his legs remembered their intended function and began to bear his weight. He managed to pry his hand loose from the saddle horn. He put a hand on the horse's neck, surprised that the animal was quivering and soaked with sweat. He rubbed the neck, reaching higher with each stroke, finally rubbing around the base of his ears. A sense of the horse's fear seemed to be telegraphed through his touch. He could feel the horse's fear! Instinctively he responded to it. He willed his hands and voice to communicate reassurance, while remembering to keep a tight grip on the reins with one hand.

The horse snorted two or three times, then began to settle down. Ian found himself crooning to him, 'It's all right, fella. You tried. You done your best. You just didn't get me dumped, did you, huh? You're just as scared o' me as I was o' you, ain't you? We're gonna be friends now, you an' me, ain't we? You're gonna be a good horse, I'm guessin'.'

As he continued to croon softly to the frightened animal, it settled down visibly. Its breathing slowed. Its ears lifted. Its nostrils lost the wide flare. It tossed its head again, but more gently than before, and began a strange chewing motion.

'Lookee that!' one of the hands on the fence exclaimed. 'One ride an' the dang horse is already takin' to 'im.'

Ian had no idea what that meant, but he decided it was a good thing.

Another voice said, 'He's a natural, that kid is.'

'Hey, Chet, I think you just hired a bronc buster to take Lyle's place.'

Once again, Ian didn't know what that meant, or who Lyle was. He just suddenly wanted to cry, and he had no idea why. He just knew he really liked this animal he had been so terrified of half an hour before. He didn't know it yet, but he had just run headfirst into his calling.

8

'That was quite a show you put on!'

'Huh?' Ian looked quizzically at one of the Two-Bar hands no more than two or three years older than he.

'I said that was quite a show.'

Ian shook his head. 'That was tryin' to stay alive,' he argued.

Casey Forester grinned. 'Oh, he wouldn't likely kill you,' he stated. 'As a matter o' fact, once a horse dumps you, he'll most generally try his dangdest to keep from steppin' on you. Unless he's an outlaw, o' course. Once in a while there's a horse that's just plumb bad.'

'Sorta like people, huh?'

Casey chuckled appreciatively. 'Yup. Just like that.'

'To be honest,' Ian confessed, 'I didn't think I had a chance to ride 'im.'

'Neither did anyone else.'

'They were all sittin' there on the

fence like they was at a circus or somethin'.'

'They were.'

'It wasn't no circus from where I was sittin'.'

'The only thing more fun than watchin' some green hand get bucked off is watchin' some fella that thinks he's hot stuff get stood on his head.'

'Or killed.'

'Aw, nobody much ever gets killed, just gettin' bucked off. Oh, I s'pose it could happen, but it ain't likely. We all get bucked off once in a while.'

Ian stared. 'You're puttin' me on. I seen you ride. You ride like you an' the horse are all one critter.'

'Yeah, but I been doin' it since afore I could walk, I reckon. I growed up on a horse.'

'The only horse I ever rode much is Speck, my geldin'. An' he was already broke to ride when I got 'im.'

'Yeah! That's exactly what I mean. I don't know nobody that ever rode the first bronc he ever forked, an' rode 'im plumb to a standstill. I ain't never even heard of anyone doin' that. You're a natural, you are. A natural-born bronc buster.'

'I dunno 'bout that. You seem to know everythin' there is to know around here. I feel like an idiot.'

'You ain't no idiot. You're just green. I'll tell you what. You let me teach you what you don't know 'bout ridin' an' ropin' an' all that, then maybe we can throw in together an' do bronc bustin' insteada just plain cowboyin'.'

Ian continued to stare. Finally he said, 'Why?'

'Better money. Bronc busters get paid by the head. The harder we work, the more money we make. We can make five or six times what reg'lar cowboys make. Besides, we'd get to stay in the bunkhouse, summer an' winter. Eat reg'lar meals in the chow hall. Work when we want to, an' go to town when we want to. Nobody tellin' us what to do, just as long as we get the horses broke that whatever ranch we're on wants broke.'

Ian mulled the idea over for a long time, staring off across the sage at the looming mountains. 'Why me?' he asked.

Casey grinned. 'Couple o' reasons. You're good to be around. You don't pretend none. You're just who you are. An', like I said, you're a natural-born bronc buster. If a man's gonna make a livin' at that, he needs a partner he can depend on. We'll split everythin' fifty-fifty. If one of us gets busted up enough he can't work for a while, the other one takes up the slack, an' it's still fifty-fifty.'

Ian looked the other man over with a much more careful appraisal than he had before. He took note of the breadth of the other's shoulders, the thickness of his chest, the bulging muscles of both arms and legs. It was the eyes that fascinated him the most. They looked older, wiser somehow than they should, considering the other's age. Certainly older and wiser than he felt himself to be.

'You think anybody'd hire us?'

'Nope. Not yet. But if you let me teach you what I know, as much of a natural as you are, in another six months or so outfits will be offerin' us the jobs.'

Ian gave it another long moment of thought. At last he nodded and said, 'You're on.'

As they shook hands, Ian felt as if something great and momentous had just occurred. A strange feeling — not a shudder, not a chill — just strange and different, swept across him for an instant and was gone.

Ian got bucked off for the first time less than a month later. He was riding a horse that he had been working for a couple weeks, and was responding well. When a cottontail burst out of a clump of sagebrush, the horse began bucking furiously instead of shying sideways. Out of position and paying less than careful attention, Ian was left sitting on the air where the horse had been an instant before. He landed with a crash in the same patch of sagebrush from which the rabbit had scampered.

Riding at a gallop, Casey roped the frightened horse and led it back to Ian. 'Now why'd he blow up on me like that?' Ian lamented.

Casey grinned. 'Plumb natural thing to do when a half-broke horse gets spooked,' he said. 'You forgot to hang on to the reins, though.'

'I wasn't even thinking about hanging on to anything.'

'Yeah, but you gotta always hang on to the reins, no matter what happens. Even if one piles you up in a patch o' cactus, you gotta hang on to them reins. Otherwise, you're gonna be afoot in the middle o' nowhere, sometime. A man can die tryin' to get back home afoot.'

Gingerly assessing his bangs and scrapes, Ian digested the information. It was just one in what seemed like an endless flow of lessons from the more seasoned cowboy.

'Turn your wrist like this when you throw your loop, if you're tryin' to front-foot somethin'. Thataway the loop just curls around in front o' the leg and they step right into it.'

'Get that rope dallied quick, just as soon as you jerk it to close your loop.'

'Don't hold the rope like that when you're dallyin'. You'll get a finger in between the wraps, and you'll lose the finger.'

'Watch the ears on the calves. When one's got his ears droopin', he's feelin' sick, an' you need to rope 'im so you can doctor 'im.'

'Quit tryin' to guide your horse when you're cuttin' stuff out of a bunch. If he's got cow in 'im, he'll know where that critter's goin' afore you do. Just ride loose an' let him work it away from the others.'

'If a horse starts tossin' his head up in your face, just run a light rope from the chin strap on your bridle underneath 'im, and fasten it to the cinch. Then he can't do that, and he'll quick learn he ain't supposed to.'

'Even when you're in a hurry, take

the time to curry him everywhere the saddle's gonna ride. Even a small burr will make him sore in a hurry.'

'Get off an' lead your horse up the really steep hills. He'll wear out afore the day's over if you just sit there like a sack o' spuds an' make him do all the work.'

'When you're lookin' over a bunch o' mares, an' the stud acts like he's gonna come after you, just shake out about six or eight feet o' rope an' keep whirlin' it in a big circle, out beside you, between you an' him. There's somethin' about that even a ringy stud won't try to get past.'

The lessons never stopped, it seemed, and Ian absorbed them like a sponge. He overheard Casey tell Chet, 'I ain't never had to tell 'im the same thing twice.'

It was only five of the six months Casey had predicted when their first offer came. The Triple T Ranch offered six dollars a head for them to break thirty head of three- and four-year-olds.

Casey countered with ten dollars a head. They settled on eight.

When they told Plover what they were doing and drew their wages, Ian tried to buy the first horse he had broken on the Two-Bar. He had named him Adam, because he was the first bronc he had tamed. He had also made something of a pet of him. He had begun to experiment with trick rides Casey or other hands suggested. He learned everything Casey suggested, and improvised a number of other stunts.

'We gotta show you two off now,' Casey announced.

'Whatd'ya mean?'

'When we go to town, you gotta do all them stunts out in the street.'

'Like some hot-stuff show-off?'

'Yeah. But I'll announce you, so folks will be watchin.'

'I ain't gonna do stunts just to show off.'

'Call it business.'

'How's that business?'

'If we show off what you can do with a horse that started out a raw bronc just a few months ago, word'll get around you're a real bronc buster. If we want all the ranches around to hire us, we gotta get folks to talk about us.'

Little by little he wore down Ian's resistance to the idea. Finally they rode into Chugwater to carry out Casey's plan. Ian had more knots in his stomach than he'd felt since his first ride.

Casey strode into the Silver Dollar Saloon and stopped just inside the door. 'Hey, you fellas wanta see a guy ridin' a horse like they do in them circuses? You gotta see this.'

He stepped back, halfway out the door in obvious invitation. Several of the saloon's patrons looked back and forth at each other, then almost as one they rose and trooped to the door. After all, they were in town, or at least in the saloon, for a little of the diversion and pleasure that was scarce in that country. There was no chance they'd sit inside and ignore something that offered either one or both.

When most of them were outside, looking around to see what was promised to be so exciting, Casey let out a shrill whistle.

At the signal, Ian rode into sight at the end of the street, standing up on the saddle, the reins tied together and looped over the saddle horn. He whirled a large loop of his lariat as he rode. At a word, the horse lifted his pace to a gallop. As he did, Ian kept the loop of his lariat getting bigger and bigger. Right in front of the Silver Dollar, he swung the loop in front of the horse. He and the horse galloped through the loop, and he swung it back up from behind them, keeping it swinging, reducing the size of the loop to manageable size again.

An appreciative whoop went up from several of the observers. Other people up and down the street began to step outside or to peer out windows to see what the ruckus was about.

At the end of the street he dropped into the saddle, turned the horse around, and started back. Casey strode out into the street and threw his hat on the ground, with the brim on top. Still swinging his lariat, Ian galloped back up the street. He leaned to one side, hooked his right foot on the saddle horn, and leaned out and down to snatch the hat from the ground with his left hand, all the while keeping the loop of his lariat spinning with his right hand.

Turning around again at the other end of the street, he coiled the rope and secured it to the loop on his saddle. Then he again climbed up on to the saddle, standing with his feet on the saddle's seat. He placed Casey's hat on the horse's head, then placed one of his hands on the cantle, the other on the pommel, and raised himself to a vertical position, with his feet straight in the air. As they passed the Silver Dollar, he shifted his weight so he was standing on only the hand that rested on the saddle horn. With the other hand he swept Casey's hat off the horse's head and sailed it to Casey as they loped past. Casey stepped out and ducked his head so that the hat would land on his head.

Applause broke out all up and down the street. 'That's the horse nobody on the Two-Bar could break,' Casey lied. 'He took him from a raw bronc nobody could ride to doin' all that in just four months.'

At least the second half of the claim was true, Casey reasoned. And nobody else had ridden that horse, so maybe they couldn't have. It just might be all true.

Back in the saddle, Ian whirled the horse around and loped back. He stopped right in front of the Silver Dollar, turning the horse to face the grinning bunch that comprised that part of his audience. At his word the horse put one front foot out in front, bent the other front leg and lowered his head, bowing to the watchers. They whooped and hollered in approval.

As the chorus of questions and comments surged, Ian wheeled the horse and rode on down to the livery barn and ducked inside, desperate to be out of the public eye and to stop being the center of everyones attention.

'Quite a show,' Harvey Mulkey drawled, his voice fairly dripping with sarcasm. 'I thought you wanted to learn how to be a cowboy, not some tin-horn show-off.'

Ian's ears burned. 'I, we, I mean, that is, well, uh, me'n Casey wanta get jobs breakin' horses. He convinced me the way to get word around was to show off the stuff we can get horses to do.'

The horse also knew that Ian kept treats of one kind or another in his pockets most of the time. He kept nuzzling him, bumping him harder and harder with his nose as Ian ignored him. He fished in his vest pocket and pulled out a piece of rock candy. He held it out in the palm of his hand. The horse grabbed it instantly and began crunching it.

'Well, you got a way with horses, I'll give you that,' Mulkey conceded. 'Do you want 'im put up now, or you gonna do another show for your admirin' crowd? Maybe pass the hat the second time around?'

Ian felt himself turn bright red. 'I done all I got the stomach to do for one day,' he groused. 'Now I gotta go over to the Silver Dollar an' act like I wanta answer all the questions about how I teach a horse to do that.'

The stunt succeeded in catching the attention of both the hands and owners of other ranches. At Casey's urging, Ian nearly always rode that horse to town, and delighted people with his acrobatics. He was self-conscious about doing it at first, but Casey insisted it was one of the things that would bring them good-paying jobs breaking and training horses. The more of it he did, the more people on the street would call out requests for him to do certain stunts. It worked beyond anything he thought possible.

116

He became a celebrity of sorts.

Half a dozen times he had nearly fallen in the middle of a stunt, though. He kept catching a fleeting glance of someone who was startlingly familiar. Every time he turned for a better look, whoever it was had gone. It niggled at the corners of his mind, though, with a sense of alarm he could not identify.

Because he and the horse became locally famous together, and because he had grown so attached to the animal, he really wanted to buy him. He offered Plover three times what he was worth to the rancher, but Plover was adamant. 'As long as that horse is here, you boys'll be back from time to time, and I've always got a few horses that need a little work.'

They settled quickly into the life of bronc busters, moving from ranch to ranch as they were hired. The pair had been at the Triple T Ranch for less than a month when Brick Ferguson brought the news. They'd had a good day working the horses, and had just turned them into the corral with feed and water, when Brick rode in. They knew from his expression he was the bearer of bad tidings.

'Hey, Brick, you're a ways from home.'

'Yeah. I, uh, just wanted to ride over and let you know what happened.'

Ian's heart dropped, because the cowboy was watching him, not Casey. 'What happened?' he asked, trying to keep the squeak out of his voice.

'Somebody shot your horse.'

Ian felt as if someone had slugged him in the stomach. All sounds faded from his consciousness. He stared at the familiar face of the Two-Bar hand. 'What? Adam?' he croaked.

Brick didn't repeat what he had said. Instead he said, 'A couple o' the boys heard the shot. It was over that hill right west o' the place, just ahead o' dark, yesterday. They didn't think a whole lot about it. Just sorta wondered who was over there, and figured whoever it was must be shootin' at a coyote or somethin'. This mornin' Chet sent Tuffy an' Murphy out to run the remuda into the corral, an' they saw him lyin' there.'

Ian's mind flew through a gamut of emotions. Disbelief. Fury. Grief. Confusion. Back to a blind, seething rage, seeking a focus but totally adrift, unable to find any. All he could think to say was, 'Why? Was it an accident?'

Brick shook his head. 'No, it for sure wasn't no accident. We seen where someone rode up, got off his horse, used a tree to steady his gun. Shot 'im right behind the front leg, from not more'n a hundred yards. Then he rode off fast.'

Casey said, 'Somebody rode to the ranch, just to find that horse and shoot him?'

'Sure looks that way.'

'You ain't made any enemies that bad have you, Ian?'

Ian shook his head. 'Only one I can even think of at all is Tub. I knocked him down the day I got to town.'

119

Casey and Brick both shook their heads. Brick said, 'Tub gets kinda mouthy when he's had a few too many to drink, but he wouldn't never do anythin' like that.'

Casey nodded his agreement. 'Naw, he wouldn't do that. Not in a hundred years.'

'So who did? And why?' Ian insisted.

Neither man had so much as a guess to offer. Even through the dark haze of his grief, Ian recognized that someone hated him. Really hated him. Hated him enough to kill a fine horse in cold blood, just to hurt him. He also recognized that sooner or later, he would learn who, and why, and that person would answer to him.

9

'Wanta do some target practicin'?'

Ian's head jerked up. He studied the face of his friend. 'Why?'

Casey shrugged, overdoing the effort to seem casual. 'Oh, just thought we might. We've pretty well got everything we wanted to do today already done. Besides, I ain't had a chance to teach you anything about usin' a gun.'

Ian started to tell his friend he continually found opportunity to practice that when nobody else was around, but he bit his tongue. Instead he said, 'You think you can teach me somethin' about that?'

Casey shrugged. 'I ain't no gunman, but I'm fair to middlin' with a gun. I ain't never seen you shoot.'

'Well, I 'spect I'd just as well learn what you can teach me.'

'I got some cans I had the cook save

for me. I'll go set 'em up.'

Ian kept a perfectly straight face. 'I gotta go over to the bunkhouse for a minute, then we'll do that. Where you settin' 'em up?'

'Oh, I thought down in the bottom o' that little gully behind the bunkhouse'd be good. Then if you shoot too wild, you won't shoot the windows outa the boss's house.'

'Well, that sounds like a good idea,' Ian agreed.

Fifteen minutes later he walked up to where his friend was waiting. Casey turned to him and started to say something, then stopped, his mouth hanging open. His eyes were riveted on the .45 tied down on Ian's right leg. Both the holster and the exposed gun butt bore witness to a good bit of use. 'Where'd you get that?' he demanded.

'Oh, a friend gave it to me. He thought I might need it sometime.'

'Can you use it?'

'Oh, sorta.'

'Then why do you always wear the other one?'

Ian shrugged. 'It ain't in the way as much when I'm workin' horses. Besides, wearin' that one the way I do, folks don't wonder whether I'm some sorta gunfighter.'

Casey grinned. 'You think they might make that mistake, huh?'

Ian shrugged again. 'Not likely, I s'pose. I don't know. I might be able to shoot as good as you, though.'

Casey's grin broadened. 'You think so? Well, to make it interesting, we could bet a little money on that.'

'Aw, you'd just take my money.'

'Prob'ly. Like I said, I ain't no gunman, but I'm pretty good. Can you hit anything?'

Ian shrugged yet again. 'Yeah, sometimes. Most o' the time, actually. Matter o' fact, I guess I'd be willin' to bet five dollars that I can hit one o' them cans afore you can.'

'You're on. Draw and shoot?'

'Draw and shoot.'

'What'll we use for a signal?'

'I'll toss a rock up in the air, behind us. When we hear it hit the ground, that'll be the signal.'

Casey crouched in readiness. 'You toss the rock. This is gonna be the easiest five bucks I ever made.'

Ian picked up a good-sized rock and threw it as high as he could, in an arc well behind them, out of sight. When it hit the ground, Casey grabbed his gun.

His gun was less than halfway out of the holster when Ian's gun barked. One of the cans flew into the air. A second shot tore through it while it was still airborne. A third hit it an instant later. When the can finally settled on the ground, it had six holes in it.

Casey was still standing with his gun half out of the holster. He stared, open-mouthed, first at the can, then at Ian, then at the can again.

Ian calmly ejected the spent brass from his .45 and replaced it with fresh rounds. His face still without expression, he said, 'I 'spect you can teach me some things that'll help me be able to do some better.'

Casey stared at him, totally speechless.

Ian couldn't keep the hint of a smile from the corners of his mouth. 'I think you owe me five dollars.'

'I owe you a pitchfork in the butt,' he said. 'As long as we been friends, and you ain't never told me you're a sure-enough gunman? You ain't just fast; you've gotta be the fastest man with a gun that I've ever seen in my life! You put six shots in that can before I could get my gun outa the holster. And I ain't slow. At least I ain't that slow! Are you runnin' from the law? Is that how come you don't want nobody to know how good you are with a gun?'

Ian shook his head. 'I ain't runnin' from the law or nothin'.'

'Where'd you learn to shoot like that?'

'That friend I mentioned. He was a gunsmith. I worked for him. He taught me to use it, and I've done a lot o' practicin'. But he told me if I wore the other gun, and wore it the way I do, I wouldn't have people wantin' to find out if they was faster'n me an' all that stuff.'

'I don't think there is anyone faster'n you.'

Ian shook his head again. 'That's one o' the things Everett drummed into me. No matter how fast anyone is, he said, there's always gonna be somebody come along that's faster. I don't want to be a gunfighter: I want to be a bronc buster. Sooner or later, I want to be a rancher.'

Casey stared at his friend for a long moment. 'This is gonna take some gettin' used to.'

'It's your turn. Go ahead an' take a shot at the cans,' Ian said. 'When I clap my hands, go for your gun.'

Casey again crouched in readiness. When Ian clapped his hands, the older cowboy's hand streaked to his gun. He whipped it from its holster and fired off six rapid rounds. He hit four of the six cans at which he was aiming. He reholstered the gun and looked at his friend for approval.

Ian scratched the back of his neck, obviously uncomfortable. Up to now, Casey had been the undisputed leader of the team, fountain of wisdom and experience, and had felt in all ways superior. Ian struggled with his sudden need to assume that position when it came to skill with a gun.

He cleared his throat and said, 'Well, if you want, I can show you some things you're doin' wrong. You missed two outa six, and to be real honest, you ain't very fast.'

'I'm fast enough,' Casey argued.

'I gotta be honest with you, Casey. You ain't fast enough to beat my grandma in a stand-up gunfight. But I can teach you. You've taught me a ton o' stuff about cowboyin'. I can maybe pay you back by teachin' you how to draw a whole lot quicker'n you do. An' how to shoot straight, too.'

After a long pause Casey said, 'Fair

enough. I guess I got a lot to learn.'

'You got five bucks you need to pay me, first thing,' Ian grinned.

The roles were reversed then, for a long while, as Ian passed on the endless lessons he had learned from the gunsmith who had become a father figure to him.

'Never watch a man's hands, if you're gonna have to draw against him. He'll draw and shoot you before you can react if you do. Watch his eyes. They'll tell you when he's gonna draw.'

'How?'

'I ain't sure, but you'll figure it out when we practice. Maybe it's the eyes just get a little bit wider, just before he draws. Maybe there's somethin' in there behind the eyes that you can see that you don't know you're seein'. But if you practice, you can see it, every time.

'Never let the other guy pick the time an' place, if you can help it. Try to have the sun behind you, especially if it's early in the mornin' or late in the afternoon.

'Look around all the time, 'cause hired gunmen don't usually take chances they don't hafta take. There ain't no such thing as a fair fight. Chances are he'll have someone off to the side somewhere with his gun already out, or with a rifle, waitin' to shoot you so it'll look like the other guy just beat you to the draw.

'Always check twice to make sure you got the loop off of the hammer, when you think you even might need to use your gun.

'Don't never try to draw with gloves on. If you're wearin' gloves, learn to jerk your hand outa your glove as you reach for your gun.'

The lessons went on and on, seeming to Casey as endless as the lessons on being a cowboy that he had imparted to Ian. As time went on, Casey's speed and accuracy improved markedly.

10

'Get a letter from your girl?'

'Yup. Five of 'em.'

Casey grinned. 'Five of 'em? Five letters, all at one time?'

Ian squirmed, uncomfortable with displaying emotion, even to his closest friend. 'Well, it takes a while for 'em to get here, you know. I send 'er one every time we're here in town where I can mail one, an' lots o' times they sorta pass each other on the way, you know.'

'Yeah, but five letters!'

'She even comes right out an' says she loves me. Signs 'em, 'With Love'.'

'Sounds like she's gettin' kinda antsy, waitin' for ya.'

Ian nodded emphatically. 'She is, but she's waitin'. I promised her I'd come back for her just as soon as I had a place an' some way to support her.'

'Well, we're gettin' closer.'

'Yeah. We got a lotta jobs lined up already.'

'More horses to do than we can get done in a year and a half.'

Ian gripped the letters, frowning. 'Yeah, that's true. But if I'm gonna get to where I can go back for Corky, I gotta have a place to live. You an' me can live in bunkhouses or most anywhere, but if I bring her out here . . . I mean *when* I bring her out here, we gotta have a house.'

'You could homestead. There's spots along Richeau Crick, or South Fork, or Middle Fork, that'd make nice home sites.'

'I been thinkin' about that. Especially up there along Middle Fork. Nice country up there. You could homestead next up or down the crick, then we could bring horses there to break, insteada goin' around to the ranches.'

Casey pursed his lips thoughtfully. 'Might work. Gotta give that some thought.'

As they talked, Ian had ripped open

131

one of the letters and begun to read. He stood up straight suddenly and swore. It was the first time Casey had heard him do so.

'What's wrong?' he demanded.

Ian's eyes darted up and down the street. He looked back at the letter. Then he swore again.

Casey opened his mouth to repeat his enquiry, but shut it instead, waiting.

Finally Ian looked at his friend. 'It just clicked.'

'What just clicked?'

'You know I been tellin' you I keep seein' someone watchin' me, an' I can't never get no more'n a glimpse, never enough to see who it is?'

'Yeah, but I thought you was just seein' ghosts or somethin'. Up until your horse got shot, that is.'

Ian's eyes went hard. 'Yeah. That too. It just all clicked.'

'So tell me.'

Ian took a deep breath. 'Way back when I was a kid in school, there was a big kid and his three friends that used to beat up on me all the time. That gunsmith I told you about? Well he took me under his wing. Taught me how to stand up to 'em. Taught me how to fight. I ended up whippin' 'em, an' makin' 'em leave me alone.'

'You whipped all four of 'em?'

Ian nodded. 'I got whipped up on somethin' awful doin' it, but I kept after 'em till they hollered 'Uncle', an' promised to leave me alone.'

'So you took care of it.'

'Well, the one guy . . . the leader . . . his name was O'Toole . . . His pa came after me, and I 'spect he mighta kilt me, but that gunsmith forced him to back down. He convinced O'Toole's pa that if any of 'em bothered me any more, he'd answer to him. So Shaun — his name was Shaunnessy O'Toole — he hated my guts, but his old man wouldn't let him do nothin'. Him an' his buddies up an' left Sioux City a little over a year afore I did.'

'So what's that got to do with now?'

'He's here.'

'What?'

'O'Toole's here.'

'In Chugwater?'

'Not in town. Somewhere around here. Corky was talkin' to someone that one of his buddies writes to, from time to time. He mentioned Chugwater. She told me to watch out for him.'

'So you think that's who you keep seein'?'

'I'm sure of it. It didn't register, except that the guy looked real familiar, 'til Corky told me he was here. As soon as I read that, it all just fell into place. There ain't no doubt.'

'So he's seen you an' he knows you're here.'

'Yup.'

'An' he's stayin' hid from you.'

'Seems that way.'

Casey's eyes widened suddenly. 'Do you think he . . . ?'

He didn't need to finish the thought. Ian was already thinking the same thing. 'He wouldn't even think twice about killin' a horse just to get even with me,' he declared. 'It's gotta be him, just as sure's anything.'

Casey shook his head. It was beyond his grasp that anyone could carry a childhood grudge that long, or act on it that viciously. He said as much.

'You don't know Shaun,' was all Ian said.

'So what're you gonna do?'

Ian took a deep breath. 'Well, I'm gonna do one thing you been tryin' to get me to do. Wear the other gun. All the time. Keep my eyes open. Ask around. I'll find 'im, sooner or later.'

'We gotta start at the Diamond J tomorrow.'

'Yeah.'

'Maybe they'll have heard somethin'.'

'Yeah.'

'You want me to ask around town?'

Ian thought about it. 'No. The less we say, the better. Up to now he don't think I know he's in the country around here at all. The longer we keep it that way, the better.'

'Watch your back.'

Ian grinned suddenly. 'You watch my back. Ain't that what friends are for?'

Casey didn't return the grin. He was clearly too worried to smile about anything just then.

'Anyway,' Ian dismissed the matter, 'I gotta read all these letters from Corky, then I gotta get a letter written back to her.'

'OK. I need a drink. I'll see you later.'

'Really? I thought maybe you'd be stoppin' over to have supper with the Clausens.'

Up to then Ian hadn't mentioned the fact that Casey was spending more and more time with Iva Clausen, daughter of the owners of the Chugwater Mercantile Store.

Casey's face flamed red. 'I didn't know you knew I was seein' her.'

'She seems like a fine girl,' Ian offered. 'Too fine for a smelly old bronc buster, I'd think.'

Casey grinned, suddenly at ease with his friend knowing his secret. 'Aw, I clean up pretty good when I've a mind to. I even wash my neck afore I come to town.'

'Yeah, I noticed. It took me a while to figure out why your clothes was all washed up so nice an' smellin' sweet every time we came to town. You never take 'em over to Ching Lee like I have to, if I don't wanta wash 'em myself.'

'He'll likely be leavin'.'

'Who?'

'Ching.'

'Why?'

'Just 'cause there ain't no other Chinese around here. I heard there's gettin' to be lots of 'em over at Rock Springs, where they're minin' coal.'

Their talk drifted idly until Ian's impatience to read Corky's letters prodded him to a place of seclusion.

11

There was no real explanation for the knot in his stomach. The ache he had felt since learning his beloved horse had been shot had never left. It had settled into a familiar, hard knot in his gut, like a rock that wouldn't digest. It cast a shadow over even the sunniest of days.

The letters he had received from Corky should have dispelled the sense of portending gloom. Instead, it gave it a form and a face. It made every shadow, every shifting shape he glimpsed from the corner of an eye, every unexpected sound, a sense of threatening evil.

The easy, sometimes ribald camaraderie that was part of every ranch crew kept the morbid sense of impending trouble at bay. When they were busy breaking horses, or at the end of the day around the supper table or in the bunkhouse, the lighthearted banter helped dispel it.

It was different on the Diamond J. It would have been hard to describe, but they felt it, even when they first rode into the yard.

Ian and Casey showed up in mid-morning, the day they were supposed to arrive. They were the closest thing to celebrities the area boasted. Always, every hand on a ranch knew when they were expected. Usually they would have scheduled the work so most of them could watch the topping off of the first few head of horses the rancher wanted broken.

Predictably, one of the first ones would be a horse several of the hands had tried to ride, and been unsuccessful. Horses, like their riders, learned with practice. A horse that bucked particularly hard, or had a perverse and clever streak, would figure out the moves that unseated the best riders. They would perfect those moves the same way an athlete perfects trademark moves or skills.

Just as predictably, nobody was about to share what those moves were with a professional bronc buster. If he knew what that signature move was likely to be, he could be prepared. If he were prepared, they'd be cheated out of seeing a professional fail to ride the horse they couldn't ride.

That always lent something of a carnival air to the day a professional bronc buster went to work on a place. Everyone on the ranch knew which one was 'the' horse. Sometimes it would be the first one the bronc buster topped. Often it wasn't, because they knew he'd be expecting the first one to be a tough one. If they were especially subtle, they'd watch closely as he topped off the first two or three, then appear to lose interest and start drifting away from the round breaking-corral. If it worked, and he was caught off guard, he would be more likely to get 'stacked up'. As soon as he mounted 'the' horse, they would all rush back to the top rail of that corral to watch the action.

It was different on the Diamond J.

When Ian and Casey rode into the yard, they garnered only casual glances. There was no air of expectation. There was none of the usual measuring surveys of them as the hands weighed their chances against 'the' horse. Most of the time there was money bet for and against the likelihood of a successful first ride of that animal, so the visual assessments were more than casual. Much of the time, the first day on the ranch felt like being on a stage, studied by a panel of judges.

It was different on the Diamond J.

There would usually be a good-sized remuda of horses within sight of the main ranch yard. The regular hands would have gathered them and herded them in close, just as a courtesy to the bronc busters. Here, there were no horses in sight, except those that were obviously part of regular working strings. Those in sight all bore indications of regular saddle wear.

Things were very different on the Diamond J.

Nearly always, they were met by the foreman upon arrival. Nobody stepped forward this time to greet them. They looked at each other, then both shrugged in unison. They opted to ride to the main house, sitting their horses before the front door, as custom required. In less than a minute the door opened, and Cy Camphor stepped out on to the porch. Both men noted instantly that he wore both .45s on his hip and carried a rifle, even on his own front porch.

'Howdy, Mr Camphor,' Casey offered.

A flash of recognition lit the rancher's eyes. 'Oh! Now I recognize you boys. I guess I only met you once before. Took me a minute.'

'We was supposed to show up today.'

'Yup. You're right on time.'

He turned slightly away from them, facing the horse barn, and bellowed, 'Bull!'

In the space of half a minute or so a man stepped to the door of the barn. He looked across the yard, sized up the situation, and started walking their way. It was instantly obvious where he got the nickname. At a couple inches over six foot, he was built like a barrel. He walked with his large head thrust forward, his huge arms swinging in time with his strides. As he approached, he said in a startlingly mild and friendly voice, 'Aha! You boys must be the bronc stompers.'

'Yeah, 'cept when we're the ones gettin' stomped,' Casey replied with a grin.

'Well, step down, fellas.'

Relieved to finally receive the invitation that was habitually given before anything else was said, both men stepped to the ground. Bull extended a hand to each in turn, giving each a handshake that did justice to his handle.

'Boys, this here's my foreman, Bull Cassidy,' Camphor explained. 'Beggin' your pardon, but I ain't sure I remember you boys' names.'

'Casey Forester.'

'Ian Hennessy.'

'Both German, huh?' Bull asked with a perfectly straight face.

'Only on my pa's side,' Ian replied instantly. 'Ma was a Scandahoovian.'

'Ah, that explains the dark hair. All them Scandahoovians got hair as black as Kelsey's.'

Both men frowned in confusion. 'Who's Kelsey?'

Bull grinned. 'Kelsey O'Grady. He's one of our top hands. Colored boy. Blacker'n the ace o' spades, he is, with about the most Irish name you ever heard. Fine cowboy in spite o' the name.'

'Well whatd'ya know!' Ian replied instantly. 'For once I'm not gonna be the most un-Irish-lookin' Irishman on the place.'

'You are short a few freckles,' Bull conceded.

'Them horses don't look much like

they need busted,' Casey commented, nodding toward the scattered horses.

'Naw, we ain't got the green ones gathered up yet. Sorry about that. I guess you boys'll hafta do your own gatherin' this time. I'll send Kelsey out with you in the mornin'. He'll show you where they're at, an' help you run 'em in close. There's a fenced-off pasture up behind the barn a ways you can run 'em into. It's a good hundred acres with a seep spring, so you won't hafta waste any o' your time worryin' about feed an' water.'

'That'll be fine with us,' Ian assured him. 'We don't mind roundin' 'em up ourselves.'

Camphor nodded. 'Good enough. You boys can unload your stuff in the bunkhouse an' make yourselves to home.'

Both men mounted up without another word and rode to the bunk-house. Camphor and his foreman stood talking together in tones too low for them to hear as they rode away, but they both had the distinct feeling they were the center of the conversation.

The bunkhouse reception was as out of the ordinary as their initial welcome to the ranch. All of the hands seemed on edge. Several times they were sure they were again the topic of quiet conversations, but nothing overt was said.

When most of the crew was back in the bunkhouse after supper, Casey broached the subject. 'The place seems sorta tense. Anythin' goin' on we oughta know about?' he asked to nobody in particular.

The instant looks that were exchanged confirmed what they had felt. After an awkward moment of silence, an old cowboy, with a face as brown and wrinkled as old leather said, 'We're just a wee mite suspicious of strangers.'

'Why's that?'

'Well, fact is, we been losin' stock. Cattle an' horses both.'

'Rustlers?'

'Either that or a mighty sudden epidemic o' strayin'.'

Ian glanced around at the faces of the crew. There was a hardness in their stares that made it perfectly clear he and Casey were not above suspicion.

'There's always a little bit o' that, it seems,' Casey observed. 'I take it this is more than a little bit.'

'It's a lot more'n a little bit.'

'Any idea who's doin' it?'

'Ain't got no proof, anyhow.'

Another awkward silence was finally broken by a freckle-faced youngster.

'You'd just as well tell 'em, Plug. They'll pick up on it pretty soon anyway.'

Several hard looks conveyed a sharp disagreement on that score. Finally Plug said, 'Well, they will now, Billy, what with you shootin' off your mouth thataway.'

'I didn't really say nothin',' the youngster insisted.

Plug glared at him a moment longer, then turned his attention back to Ian and Casey. 'They's a ranch up on Iron Mountain that's hired a hard-lookin' bunch. Old man Bennett an' his wife are an odd sort, but we didn't never think they'd do anything wrong. Trouble is, ain't nobody seen either one of 'em in a spell, so we don't know what's goin' on up there. But like I said, we ain't got no proof o' nothin'. Nobody's caught anyone with stolen stock.'

'Anybody know any o' the bad bunch?'

Plug shook his head. 'We picked up a name or two. One's a known outlaw an' gunfighter from down in the nation, named Clausen. Chad Clausen. Somebody named O'Toole seems to be part of it, too.'

Both men sat with jaws agape. It was Casey who first recovered enough to ask, 'He ain't any relation to the Clausens in Chugwater, is he?'

'Not that we know of. Why?'

Ian answered for him. 'Casey's plumb sweet on the Clausen girl. Her folks seem like mighty fine folks. Honest as the day is long. They run the mercantile store in town.'

'That's where I heard that name!' one of the hands exclaimed. 'I thought it was familiar, but I didn't make the connection.'

'I know the Clausens in town,' Plug interjected. 'There ain't no way they'd be tied into anything like this.'

'What's O'Toole's first name?' Ian asked, his voice betraying that it was more than a casual question.

'Why?' Plug demanded.

Ian took a deep breath. How detailed an answer did he want to give? If he held back information, it would probably be obvious. Still, he didn't want to offer his life history, either.

He rubbed the back of his neck, pondering his answer. 'Well,' he said finally, 'that could be a longer story than any of you wanta hear. I came out here from Sioux City, Iowa. I got a girl back there, that I write to all the time. I just found out from her the other day that one o' my worst enemies from way back in school is out in this country somewhere. His name's Shaunnessy O'Toole. He's meaner'n a snake.'

'He shot Ian's horse,' Casey inserted into the conversation.

Every eye in the bunkhouse widened in surprise and disbelief. 'Shot it out from under you?' Plug demanded.

Ian shook his head. 'I wasn't even on the place. He belonged to Plover. I wanted to buy 'im, but Amos wouldn't sell 'im to me.'

'Is that the horse you was always doin' all the tricks on?'

Ian fought back his emotions. 'Yeah. That's him.'

'I never saw a horse do some o' the things he could do,' another offered.

'Best horse a man could ask for,' Ian affirmed.

'This O'Toole shot 'im?' It was again Plug who demanded.

Ian shrugged. 'I got no proof, but it figures. It happened after me'n Casey'd gone off on our own, bronc bustin'. I'd ride back and work 'im a little every two or three weeks, so he wouldn't forget all the stuff I'd taught 'im. Someone rode out to the Two-Bar, shot him with a rifle, then just rode off again. Accordin' to the foreman, anyway. Chet Hunley checked out the tracks, afore he sent someone to tell me about it.'

Deathly silence settled over the bunkhouse. It seemed as though even the incessant wind stopped tugging at the eaves and window panes. Finally Billy asked, 'Why would he do that?'

Ian shrugged again. 'Just cuz he was mine. Just cuz he knew how much he meant to me. Just cuz he's too yellow to try to do anything face to face.'

'In that case, he's just as likely to shoot you the same way.'

'Yeah. I been thinkin' some about that.'

He had, in fact, been doing a lot of thinking about exactly that.

12

'You hear that?'

'Yeah. Sounds like somebody's movin' cattle.'

'We gotta be on Diamond J range. Plug didn't say nothin' about anybody bein' up around here.'

'He said the horses oughta be somewheres around here.'

'Them ain't horses a-bellerin'.'

'We best have a look.'

Ian, Casey and Kelsey O'Grady looked at each other for a long moment. As if moved by the same thought, they each lifted the leather loop off the hammer of their Colts, readying them for use, just in case.

They eased forward to the top of a low rise. They halted their horses where they could just see beyond by removing their hats and standing in the stirrups, without being easily seen.

Moving up the shallow draw, two cowboys were herding about two dozen head of cattle. They were conspicuously silent, eschewing the normal whooping, whistling and chirping to turn stragglers back into the bunch.

In a coarse whisper, Ian said, 'Them's Two-Bar cows.'

Moving his horse silently closer to his friend, Casey whispered back, 'Amos don't range up anywhere near here.'

'What'll we do?'

'Brace 'em.'

'Where?'

Casey looked the lay of the land over carefully. 'Over there, where the draw flattens out. We can circle around and be in them trees. When we ride outa the trees, spread out a ways, we'll have 'em where they can't cut an' run.'

'Then what do we do?'

'Tell 'em to throw up their hands.'

'And if they don't?'

'Chances are they'll go for their guns. Then you'd best be danged quick.'

'What if they do give up?'

'Then we'll tie 'em up an' take 'em back to Amos. Let him deal with 'em.'

For just a minute, Ian thought he was going to be sick. The knot in his stomach fought to rise into his throat. He swallowed it forcefully, turned his horse, and eased back down the slope out of sight and sound of the rustlers.

They trotted swiftly on a roundabout course that placed them in the trees, roughly ten yards apart. From their cover, they watched the approaching group, reassured there were only two men.

When the pair, one on either side of the bunch of cows, were about fifty feet away, the three of them rode out of the trees. 'Hold it right there, boys!' Casey yelled.

Both men let out startled yelps, swore, and grabbed for their guns.

Ian and Casey had practiced such scenarios countless times, at the older cowboy's insistence. They had done so enough times their actions had become instinctive. It was fortunate they had.

There was no time to think. There was no time to formulate a response. With near identical speed, both men drew their guns and fired in the same blur of speed. The rustlers' guns were just clear of the holsters when they were both knocked from their saddles by the lead slugs that blasted the life from their bodies.

Ian sat as still as a statue and stared. As if watching something in a different world, he watched the body of one of the rustlers hit the ground and bounce slightly. The man's gun flew several yards to one side. His hat scrunched up beneath his head. One foot flew up into the air then plopped back to the ground. He lay then without moving, both arms splayed out to the side.

He forced himself to turn to the other rustler. He lay on his side, curled up as if in sleep, his gun still gripped in his dead hand. Casey sat his horse, watching him. Except for his eyes being far too widely open, he showed no emotion.

Kelsey kept swinging his pistol from one dead rustler to the other, eyes wide, mouth hanging open.

At the burst of gunfire, the cattle had whirled and run a few steps away. They stood now, watching the three horsemen, unsure what to do.

Ian stepped from the saddle. He walked toward the man he had killed. He made a noise that sounded like something between a wheeze and a cough. He threw up suddenly, emptying the contents of his stomach on to the ground.

He spat several times, trying in vain to rid his mouth of the acrid taste of his own vomit. He started to wipe his mouth with his right sleeve, then realized he still held his revolver in that hand. He wiped his mouth on the other sleeve, reluctant to holster the weapon.

'You OK?' Casey asked.

'Yeah. Yeah. I . . . I didn't even think about what I was doin'. He grabbed for his gun, and I shot afore I even knew I was gonna draw.'

Casey nodded. 'That's why we practiced so many times,' he said. 'You ain't got time to think when someone throws down on you. You did good.'

'I didn't even get my gun out before it was all over,' Kelsey lamented.

As if he didn't hear, his voice hollow, Ian said, 'I killed him.'

'You kept him from killin' you.'

'They went for their guns.'

'Yeah, but I know him.'

As one voice, the other two said, 'You know him?'

Ian nodded his head more vigorously than was called for. 'I know him.'

'Who is he?'

'His name's Milton McCormish. Milt.'

'Where do you know him from?'

'Back home.'

'Iowa?'

'Yeah.'

'What's he doin' out here?'

'He's one of O'Toole's buddies. One of them four guys that used to pick on me, till I whipped 'em.'

'One of O'Toole's buddies,' Casey echoed thoughtfully.

'So now what do we do?'

Casey finally holstered his revolver. 'Well, I 'spect we oughta tie 'em across their saddles an' take 'em back to the Diamond J.'

'We need to take Amos's cows back to him.'

'Yeah, I 'spect so. After we haul these two to Camphor, so he can do what he wants with 'em.'

Dead men feel heavier than if they were made of gold. Maybe it was more like trying to lift two man-size bags of water, impossible to grip well. Getting them draped across their saddles was far more of a job than Ian had ever dreamed it would be. Lashing them in place with their own lariats was no problem, but it was a long ride back to the Diamond J.

Their entry into the yard there caused more of a stir than riding any bronc ever had. Camphor met them before they were fully into the ranch yard. Bull Cassidy was right behind him, backed up by half a dozen Diamond J hands.

Nobody asked any questions. They stood in silence, waiting. Kelsey explained what they had found, and what had happened. Camphor turned to the group of waiting men. 'Billy, you an' Ike take these two into town an' turn 'em over to the marshal. Tell 'im what happened.'

'He ain't gonna do nothin' about it,' Bull offered.

'No, I don't expect he will,' Cy agreed. 'He ain't got no jurisdiction outside o' town anyway. But he's the closest law around. He's gotta know.'

'Casey and Ian want to take the cattle back to the Two-Bar,' Kelsey stated.

'Makes sense to me,' Cy agreed. 'You'd just as well ride along.'

Without a word the three turned their horses and rode out of the yard.

It still seemed like some distant dream to Ian. He had confronted cattle rustlers; he had drawn his gun in a kill-or-be-killed confrontation; he had killed a man. A man he knew, or had known. It was all over in an instant of time. It felt totally and impossibly unreal.

It would become more and more real, as he relived it in dreams. It would become more and more real as he came to understand the tiny instant of time that caused it to be the rustler who died with a bullet through his heart instead of him. From time to time, he would even feel Milton's bullet tear through his own heart in one of those dreams, and wake with a start, bathed in sweat.

Little by little, he would become inured to the emotions that racked his sleep in the days and weeks that followed.

13

The owners and crew of the Rafter L proved to be just as much on edge as the Diamond J had been. Their losses to rustlers too had been great. They had also lost two hands, shot by those same rustlers, who remained unidentified.

Ian and Casey had worked on the Diamond J for just over five months, much of it through the winter. The deep snows of an exceptionally hard winter had put the brakes on most of the rustling. Besides making it difficult to drive bunches of either cattle or horses, it made it far more dangerous. Herds were moved to winter range, where they were fed daily, and, as a result, watched much more closely.

The winter snows also made it much easier to break horses. Those initial rides on each bronc were almost too easy, when the broncs were hampered by deep snow. If they did get thrown off, which happened occasionally to the best of riders, the landing was soft. Cold, to be sure, but soft.

They moved on to the Rafter L in early spring. The thaw that spring saw runoff that made the creeks and rivers exceptionally high. Cows, heavy with calf, frequently got caught in water too deep and fast to escape, and had to be rescued, or just perished. Half a dozen cowboys across the area lost either their mounts or their lives in those raging waters.

Spring also reminded Ian and Casey why they worked as bronc busters instead of regular cowhands. They pitched in and helped with the calving on the Rafter L, but they weren't obligated to do so. Neither were they obligated to be in the saddle night and day watching for cows that needed assistance, calves that needed rescuing from wolves and coyotes too eager to dine on the tender young and helpless.

They also had the privilege of going to town during a time when no regular cowboy could even think about doing so.

'You ridin' Blaze to town?' Casey queried, his eyebrows lifted.

'Sure. Why not?'

Casey pursed his lips thoughtfully. 'Oh, no reason,' he lied.

Ian stared at him, waiting for a better answer. 'You ain't plannin' on askin' me to show off like I done afore, are you?'

'You're good at it.'

'Hey! I only did all that showin' off 'cause you told me to. That was just to get started in the bronc-bustin' business.'

'Yeah, but you got him trained almost as good as you did Adam.'

'That don't mean I aim to go showin' off in town.'

Casey shrugged. 'He's your horse. I ain't tryin' to tell you what to do. A sorrel-and-white pinto like that sure stands out, though.'

'He's about the prettiest horse I've broke.'

'I'm partial to buckskins, myself.'

'Pintos ain't as common.'

The conversation continued all the way to town.

'This one trained to do all them stunts?' Harvey Mulkey, the hostler at the livery barn, asked.

'Most of 'em,' Ian conceded.

'You gonna be puttin' on one o' your big shows?'

'Naw. I only did that to drum up business for breakin' horses.'

'Seems to've worked.'

'Worked real good. I felt like a fool doin' it, but it sure enough worked. We've got jobs lined up for the rest o' the year, anyway.'

'Your sidekick come to town with you?'

'Yeah. He'll likely put his horse up at the Clausens', though.'

'Still sweet on the Clausen girl, huh?'

'He's plumb serious about her,' Ian observed. 'Savin' up his money to get married, just as soon as we can break enough horses that he can afford a wife.'

'You boys is good,' Harvey conceded.

When Ian offered no response, the stooped hostler eyed him carefully. 'Prob'ly best you not be puttin' on a show, anyhow.'

Ian frowned. 'Why's that?'

Harvey shrugged as if it mattered little. 'Just thought you might be keepin' your head down.'

'Why?'

Harvey shrugged again. 'Just thought it might be smart.'

He turned to lead Ian's horse away, but Ian stopped him. 'What do you mean? Why should I stay low?'

Harvey glanced around, assuring himself there were no extra ears listening. 'I been hearin' some whispers,' he said.

'What kind of whispers?'

'Seems you two fellas managed to get a price on your heads.'

'What? What are you talkin' about?

Why would we have a price on our heads?'

'Them two rustlers you boys shot last fall got friends, I've heard tell.'

'Who?'

Harvey spit a brown stream of tobacco juice at the bottom of a stall post. 'That I can't say. Just overheard somethin' a time or two, that the gang doin' most o' the rustlin' put up a standin' offer: five hundred dollars for anyone that plugs either one o' you two.'

The hostler looked around again, then turned back to Ian. 'Mind you, I didn't say nothin'. Whatever you mighta heard, you didn't hear it from me.'

He wheeled and led Ian's horse away, leaving him standing in the doorway, speechless.

Ian's eyes darted here and there, probing every shadow along the street. His stomach churned. He lifted the loop from the hammer of his Colt, hefted the gun and dropped it back into its holster. He took a deep breath.

Five minutes later he knocked on the door of the Clausens' house. Elise Clausen opened the door almost immediately. 'Why, Ian! Come on in. Will you join us for supper?'

Ian whipped off his hat. 'Uh, no, thanks, Mrs Clausen. Uh, I really need to talk to Casey for just a minute.'

'Well, come on in, then.'

Ian bit his lip. 'Uh, well, I mean, uh, would you mind if he just steps out here? I won't keep him more'n a minute.'

Elise stared at him. Concern and confusion furrowed her brow. 'Well, certainly. Just a minute.'

Leaving the door wide open, she disappeared into the house's interior. Less than a minute later Casey and Iva came to the door together.

Ian backed away from the door so Casey had to step out on to the porch to talk to him. Iva came along, staying close beside Casey. Ian squirmed with obvious discomfort.

'I, uh, just learned somethin' I gotta tell you,' Ian said, glancing significantly at Iva.

Casey's easy grin did nothing to dispel Ian's discomfort, as he said, 'You can tell me. I ain't got no secrets from Iva.'

Ian hesitated a long moment, then said, 'I just put my horse up at the livery barn.'

'OK.'

'Uh, well, I heard somethin'.'

'So spit it out.'

'Them rustlers went an' put a price on our heads.'

Iva gasped. Casey's eyes widened. 'What?'

'You'n me. They put a price on our heads.'

'How do you know that?'

'A fella warned me about it.'

'Who?'

'I promised I wouldn't tell anyone how I learned about it.'

'But they put a price on our heads?'

Ian nodded. 'Five hundred dollars

apiece, for anyone who kills either one or both of us.'

'Oh, Casey!' Iva breathed, grabbing Casey's arm with both hands.

'Why?'

' 'Cause we shot them two guys that was stealin' Plover's cows.'

Casey scratched his chin. He rubbed a hand across the back of his neck. He scratched his jaw. He put an arm around Iva. 'Well, it ain't likely they'll try anything in town. That'd identify 'em, as well as likely get 'em hung. We'll just have to keep our eyes open, I guess.'

The sinking feeling in Ian's gut assured him that wasn't going to be even close to adequate.

14

Ian stopped dead in his tracks. He felt the blood drain from his face. His hands felt suddenly clammy. He wiped his right hand on the front of his shirt.

Grinning wickedly, an old fear stared him in the face. He felt suddenly thirteen years old and afraid again.

He had left the Clausens' house and walked hurriedly back toward the post office to get his mail. As he stepped around the corner he had come face to face with Shaunnessy O'Toole.

'Well, lookee here,' Shaunnessy smirked. 'If it ain't the fancy show-horse rider of Chugwater himself.'

Ian was surprised that he could keep his voice calm and even. He was sure it would betray the sudden quaver he felt inside. 'I heard you was around here, Shaun,' he said.

As he spoke, the feeling of frightened

child gave way to the courage of remembering this was the person he had forced to back down. He wasn't a child any more. Shaunnessy still outweighed him. In fact, he probably outweighed him by nearly a hundred pounds now. Even so, he was no longer afraid. He straightened his back and stood as tall as his five-foot-five frame could reach.

As if oblivious to the passing years or the changes in his old victim, Shaunnessy's grin broadened. 'Havin' a hard time makin' it in a man's world?' he taunted.

'Not so's you'd notice,' Ian retorted, forcing his voice to be far more lighthearted than he felt.

'Heard you had some tough luck.'

'Everybody does, from time to time.'

'I meant about your horse. Too bad a horse that fine had to go an' get killed.'

'You wouldn't happen to know what yellow-bellied snivelin' little coward did that, would you, Shaun?'

O'Toole's grin faded only slightly. 'Well now, I might, an' I might not. That ain't the worst o' your problems, though.'

'Is that right? What's the worst o' my problems?'

'I heard tell you went an' got a price on your head.'

Ian felt the blood drain from his face again, but he kept his expression bland. 'Now where would you hear a thing like that?'

'Oh, I got ways o' knowin' what goes on in this country.'

Rising anger swept away the last dregs of Ian's hesitance. 'You ain't by chance thinkin' o' tryin' to cash in on that are you?'

An instant of doubt crossed Shaun's eyes, but the wicked grin remained plastered across his face. 'Well, now, what if I am? I could sure enough use that kinda money.'

Ian was surprised at the flat tone of his own voice as he responded. 'If you think you're quick enough or man enough, now's the perfect time for you to try.'

O'Toole's eyes darted down to the gun, inches from Ian's hand. His grin faded. His eyes returned to Ian's face. He swallowed hard. 'I can take you any day of the week,' he blustered.

'So go ahead,' Ian challenged, 'unless you're still just a blowhard like you always were.'

O'Toole's face suffused crimson. The hand hanging near his own gun flexed. He returned Ian's hard stare for several heartbeats. He swallowed again. His voice too loud and half an octave too high, he said, 'I'll pick the time an' place, ya little runt. Chances are you won't even see it comin'.'

'It'd be just like you to shoot me in the back, all right,' Ian retorted, 'what with you bein' as big a coward as you've always been.'

The red of the big man's face deepened to nearly purple. He opened his mouth twice to speak, but only made a choking sound. He wheeled and stomped away, fists clenched at his side.

'I'd watch my back mighty close, if I was you,' a voice at Ian's shoulder said.

He wheeled, unaware anyone else had approached. Tub Lemke turned his head and spat a glob of juicy tobacco into the edge of the street. 'He's low enough he just might bushwhack you,' he said.

Ian took a deep breath. 'Yeah,' was all he could think to say.

'C'mon. I'll buy you a drink,' Tub offered.

It was the first conversation between him and the pot-bellied cowboy since his first day in town. That day he had knocked the man cold for spitting on his new boots. A warm glow swept through Ian as he realized the man was offering friendship. Even so, the last thing he wanted was to drink something that would lessen his alertness and slow his hand. Besides, he still wanted to get to the post office. There would be letters from Corky waiting for him. In his vest pocket were three letters of his own to mail to her.

'Thanks, Tub,' he said, offering the man his hand. As the other took it in a strong grip, he said, 'I really need to get over to the post office right now though.'

'Fair enough,' Tub said. Then as if it were an afterthought he said, 'Oh, by the way, one o' the girls at the Silver Dollar told me that gang o' rustlers that's holed up somewhere around here have gone an' put a price on your head. You an' your bronc-stompin' buddy too.'

'Yeah. Thanks. I'd heard that.'

'Just wanted you to know about it. Like I said, watch your back.'

Without another word the man wheeled and bow-legged his way toward the Silver Dollar. It occurred briefly to Ian to wonder why a working cowboy was idling in town during calving season. He shrugged his shoulders and headed toward the post office.

15

It might as well have been a dozen miles to the post office. A dozen miles filled with canyons impossible to cross, rivers raging at flood stage and a whole tribe of hostile Indians lying in ambush, all intent on keeping him from reaching the letters that awaited him.

The sun was in his eyes. He kept looking all about, his eyes probing every shadow, the space between every building. Twice he wheeled and looked back the way he had come, certain he felt eyes staring at him from behind.

The hair on the back of his neck tingled, sending chills down his spine. He had never felt this way before. Even when he lived in terror of O'Toole and his buddies when he was a kid, he had known he would see them before they attacked. When they did attack, he would be beaten up, not killed. Now it was sudden death that stalked him.

Someone stepped into the street thirty feet in front of him. He stopped, staring hard, trying to make out the man's face. He couldn't see it clearly. The afternoon sun was squarely in his way, parked as if by design just above the man's head.

'That's far enough, Hennessy,' the man said.

'Who are you?' Ian demanded.

'Don't matter none. You ain't likely heard o' Nevada Jim anyhow.'

'Can't say that I have,' Ian responded, his mind groping desperately, at a loss to understand the situation he seemed to have been thrust into so abruptly.

'You killed a friend o' mine,' the man said.

Words of instruction that Ian had heard repeatedly from Everett Stinson, that he had, in fact, repeated often to Casey, ran unbidden through his mind. 'Never let the other guy pick the time an' place, if you can help it. Try to have the sun behind you, especially if it's early in the mornin' or late in the afternoon.'

He realized with a rush that was exactly what he had allowed to happen. He was so intent on getting to the post office he had ignored every trick of survival the gunsmith had taught him. With a name like Nevada Jim, he was almost certainly facing a professional gunfighter, an experienced and skilled killer. He was nearly blinded by the sun, and wouldn't even have had a chance against a rank amateur at that moment.

He forced himself to speak calmly, as he started to walk deliberately to his left, keeping his hand a little distance away from his gun. 'Well, now,' he said, in the friendliest voice he could manage, 'I don't know you, so I don't know who that might be. What friend are you talking about?'

The gunman was clearly confused by Ian's turning to walk over to the side of the street. He started to walk the same way, trying to keep the sun behind him, but he had lost the initial element of surprise.

Ian walked quickly to the boardwalk and stepped up on it. As soon as he had moved far enough that the sun was not directly in his eyes, he could see the other man clearly. His dress was certainly not that of a working cowboy. He wore a dark-blue silk shirt, with a silk neckerchief that nearly matched it in color. He wore a flat-topped, broad-brimmed hat, incongruous in Wyoming, where nearly every cowboy wore a tall-crowned hat, usually shaped to a peak. The name Nevada Jim suddenly made perfect sense.

The man wore a Smith & Wesson .44 low on his right thigh. Its well-worn handle was precisely positioned where his hand normally hung, the five-inch barrel ideal for a quick draw.

As he stepped up on to the sidewalk, Ian also stepped beneath the wooden awning that protected the walk from rain and snow. His suddenly unimpaired vision instantly spotted a second man, now only steps away because of his own move over to the sidewalk.

Another of Everett's oft-repeated admonitions raced through his mind. 'Look around all the time. Hired gunmen don't usually take chances they don't hafta take. There ain't no such thing as a fair fight. Chances are he'll have someone off to the side somewhere with his gun already out, or with a rifle, waitin' to shoot you so it'll look like he just beat you to the draw.'

A second thought, hard on its heels, fraught with desperation, said, 'And Casey ain't here to back me up.'

The instant the thoughts shot through his mind, Ian saw the second man already had a gun in his hand. His unexpected move over to the sidewalk had created a second of hesitation in the man on the sidewalk. His eyes flicked over toward his partner in the street, then back again. It was an instant that Ian didn't miss.

He moved without thought or plan.

He whipped his gun from its holster, firing as he did. That second man, less than six feet away from him, grunted and stepped backward.

Just as swiftly Ian swivelled his gun to the right and fired again. Nevada Jim's gun was just clearing its holster as the hot lead from Ian's gun slammed into his chest. He dropped his gun. It fired as the end of the barrel hit the ground, causing it to jump into the air and cartwheel back to earth.

Ian jerked his gun back to cover the second man, but he was already sprawling on to the ground, his feet and legs on the sidewalk, the rest of him in the street.

Ian swung his gun back to Nevada Jim again, but he was clearly dead as well.

Suddenly weak, Ian sagged back against the front of the store at his back to keep from falling.

'Are you hit?' a voice demanded.

He turned and looked into the eyes

of a man he had never met. An instant of panic faded as he noted the man was unarmed. He shook his head. 'No, I'm fine.'

'Boy, they had you set up to a fare-thee-well,' the man observed. 'One in the street and the other here on the sidewalk. How did you know the second man was here?'

Ian was spared having to answer by the running approach of Lemuel Claude, the town marshal, gun in hand. 'What's goin' on here?' he demanded.

The man at Ian's left said, 'That gunman in the street and this guy on the ground here had this young man set up just perfect,' he said. 'One of them got him looking straight into the sun, with the second man over here to make sure they had him dead to rights. I've been around this country a long time, Marshal, and I've never seen anyone get the best of a plan laid out that well.'

The marshal mulled the information

while he studied the scene. He holstered his gun. 'You know 'em?' he asked Ian then.

Ian shook his head. 'Never seen either one before. The one out there told me his name's Nevada Jim. That's all I know.'

'Any idea why they were gunnin' for you?'

Ian shook his head. 'I heard a while ago that a gang o' rustlers has put a price on my head. Might be that.'

Understanding flooded the marshal's eyes. 'You're one o' the boys that killed them two who was runnin' off Amos's stock?'

'Yeah.'

Lem nodded. 'That explains it, right enough. I heard you had a price on your head outa that deal.'

'I've heard of Nevada Jim,' the stranger who had first spoken remarked. 'He's got a long string of dead men behind him.'

'You'd know, Eli,' the marshal said. 'You two know each other?'

'Never had the pleasure,' the man said. He turned to Ian and thrust out his hand. 'Eli Canderwall,' he said.

Ian started to take the hand, then realized his gun was still in his own hand. He thrust it hurriedly into its holster and shook hands. 'Ian Hennessy,' he said.

'The bronc buster?'

'Yeah.'

'You're as fast with a gun as any I've seen,' Eli said.

'That's as fine a compliment as you'll get,' the marshal assured him. 'Eli's an old lawman. He's been down the road, over the hill, across the crick and past the next gully more'n a time or two. He runs the saddle shop here in Chugwater, nowadays.'

'How'd you get that good with a gun?' Eli demanded.

'I had a good teacher,' Ian said.

'Who might that have been?'

'A guy by the name of Stinson.'

Eli's eyes opened wide. 'Everett?'

It was Ian's turn to be stunned. 'You know him?'

'Knew him years ago. You're right. He'd be a good teacher. The best. The last I knew he went back East, hung up his gun, and married some girl back there somewhere.'

'Sioux City.'

'Sioux City? Where's that?'

'Iowa.'

The wonder in the man's voice was unmistakable. 'And you know Everett! Whatd'ya know! You learned how to handle a gun from Everett Stinson!'

'I learned a lot more than that from him. He was like a father to me, after my pa got killed in the war.'

'Is that a fact? Well what d'ya know.'

'I didn't know he'd ever actually been out West,' Ian marveled. 'I always thought he just wanted to, but never had, because his wife didn't want to leave Iowa.'

'Well, he sure enough spent time in this country,' Eli assured him. 'I rode with Everett in Kansas for a while.

There's none finer.'

The marshal interrupted the conversation with which he had already lost patience. 'Well, I guess that bunch of rustlers that are hidin' out somewhere around are about two guns less than they were when the sun came up this mornin'. I'll get the undertaker to take care of 'em, then get word to the detective.'

'The detective?' Ian responded instantly. 'What detective?'

The marshal looked at him sharply, then answered. 'The US marshal's office has appointed a range detective to try to get to the bottom o' the big rash o' rustlin' that started about a year ago. Chances are you'll be meetin' him one o' these days.'

'Don't forget to replace the caps you popped,' Eli said, as he turned to walk away.

Ian flushed as he realized he had replaced his gun in its holster without doing so. One more of Everett's seemingly interminable string of lessons he had forgotten to heed. That he had survived the day was an absolute wonder.

But he still wanted to get to the post office.

16

A flicker of movement jerked Ian's attention from the letter he was absorbing. He didn't realize for a moment that his gun was in his hand, as if of its own volition. His eyes were fixed on the gap between two buildings on the other side of the street.

A moment later a horseman emerged from between two different buildings at the far end of the street. He wheeled his horse and left town at a gallop.

'Gets easier every time,' a voice at his elbow observed.

Ian jumped and whirled toward the speaker. Eli Canderwall stood at his elbow, watching the diminishing cloud of dust the rapidly disappearing rider left behind him.

'What gets easier?' Ian demanded.

Eli nodded toward the gun that was still in Ian's hand, still pointed at the rider who was, by now, far out of pistol range. 'Grabbin' that gun any time you're a bit startled.'

Ian shoved the gun back in its holster, feeling foolish. 'Just caught a funny movement outa the corner o' my eye,' he defended.

'Yup. So your gun just automatically jumped into your hand.'

Ian felt his face flush furiously, but he could think of no comeback. Eli continued, 'Killin' a man's the same thing.'

'What do you mean?'

'Made you sick to your stomach the first time, didn't it? When you killed that fella herdin' stolen cattle, I mean.'

Ian took a deep breath. 'Yeah.'

'Didn't do that to you earlier today, though, I noticed. You shot two men today.'

'I didn't want to.'

'I know that. They came lookin' for you. It wasn't the other way 'round. But you shot 'em both. And you didn't get sick, this time.'

'No. It bothered me a lot, though.'

'Yup. Just not so much.'

'Was it supposed to?'

Eli shook his head. 'It never does. The first time you have to kill a man, it just about turns you inside out. The second time twists your gut in a knot, but not as bad. You get over it a lot quicker. The next time it'll be easier still.'

'I don't want there to be a next time.'

'You're wearin' a gun: you're faster'n a rattlesnake with it. You'll have to use it again. And again, most likely. And every time you do, it'll get a little easier. After a while, it won't even feel like you just killed another human bein' when you have to kill someone. Sorta like your soul gets calloused over, and you don't think about it much.'

'Is that the way it was with you?'

'O' course. It had to be. Otherwise, wearin' a badge, huntin' men, some-times havin' to kill 'em when I couldn't bring 'em in, I'da gone crazy. There's a limit to how many men you can watch die over and over in your dreams without losin' your mind. So you learn to not think of 'em as men any more.'

'And they never bother you after that?'

The older man's voice took on a solemn tone that echoed a bone-deep, gnawing pain that had become a familiar, never quite comfortable part of himself, like a rheumatic shoulder that always hurt. Within that tone was a somber resignation that long-term struggles with those memories would never go away. 'I didn't say that. No, sir, I surely didn't say that. They all come back, time to time. Every one of 'em. An' when they do, you wake up sweatin' like a pig an' shakin' like you takened the fever. But that ain't the point I was wantin' to make.'

Wavering somewhere between awe, fear and anger, Ian's voice was sharper than he intended. 'What point did you want to make?'

'I wanted to caution you some about how quick that gun jumped into your hand, just 'cause you caught a glimpse o' somethin' outa the corner of your eye. You gotta make sure what you're drawin' that thing on, afore you haul it outa the holster. Otherwise you'll end up like Wild Bill.'

'Who?'

'Wild Bill. Hickok.'

'You knew him?'

Eli nodded. 'I knowed him.'

'Someone shot him in the back, I heard.'

'Yup. He invited it.'

'What?'

'I said he invited it. I just don't think he could stand it any more.'

Ian frowned, making no sense of the man's words. Finally he said, 'I don't know what you're talking about.'

'Well, I'll tell you about it. My idea of the whole thing, anyway. The last stand-up gunfight Bill was in, he went and shot his best friend.'

'He did?'

Eli nodded. 'Yup. That's just exactly what he done. The gunfight was over.

The ones tryin' to kill Bill was dead. But word had got around that they was settin' Bill up, an' he was outnumbered. His best friend went runnin' to back him up. He ran out from between a couple o' buildings. Bill caught a glimpse of him outa the corner of his eye, and he just whirled and shot. Nailed him right through the heart. Afore the man hit the ground he knowed he'd just killed his best friend.'

Ian stared open-mouthed for several heartbeats. 'That'd be terrible!'

'It was all o' that. Bill never drawed his gun on another man after that. He went off up to Deadwood, tryin' to drink and gamble and whore around enough to forget. But he couldn't forget. The day he got killed, he went into that saloon and sat in on that poker game, with his back wide open to the room. He knowed good and well there was men in town who'd sworn to kill 'im. McCall wasn't the only one gunnin' for 'im. I knowed him well enough to be just as sure as I can be that it wasn't no accident, no oversight, no moment o' carelessness, that made him sit there with his back to a whole saloon full o' folks. He just wanted it over with, so he could quit rememberin'. He got what he wanted. McCall walked in, saw 'im a-sittin' thataway, walked up behind him and put a bullet through his brain.'

'Wild Bill Hickok let himself get shot in the back on purpose?'

'I'm just as sure of it as I can be.'

After a long silence, Ian said, 'So why are you telling me all this?'

Eli's piercing blue eyes bored into Ian as he spoke. 'Think about it. A couple minutes ago, if your friend Casey had run outa that space betwixt them two buildings right over there, what would you've done?'

Ian pondered the thought as the blood ran from his face. Would he have fired his gun before identifying who it was rushing into the street? If it had been Casey, would he have shot him? He shook his head vigorously. 'I — no!

I . . . I don't know! I don't think so.'

'But you ain't sure, are you?'

'I . . . I don't know how to be sure.'

'Just somethin' to keep in mind. It's a mighty fine line betwixt reactin' quick enough to stay alive, and reactin' too quick to be sure what you're shootin' at. As quick as you are, and as straight as you shoot, you better pray to God that He keeps you on the right side o' that line.'

He turned and walked away, leaving Ian feeling as if he'd just been kicked in the gut. Five minutes before, he had felt so confident of his newly tested ability and skill. Now he doubted if he would have the courage to ever use it again. But if he hesitated at the wrong moment, he would surely be dead. If he had hesitated even an instant, earlier today, he would have been dead. He felt as if he couldn't get enough air to fill his lungs, even though, he suddenly realized, he was breathing as if he had just run a mile.

He forced himself to calm down and

breathe normally.

'You look like you seen a ghost,' a familiar voice chided.

Without turning toward Casey, who had just walked up beside him, he said, 'Yeah. Sort of, I guess.'

'What's wrong?'

Ian took a deep breath. 'Nothing,' he lied, then immediately changed the subject. 'Did you see who rode outa town in a hurry?'

'No. Who?'

'It looked like O'Toole, from here. He was goin' along behind the buildings across the street. Then he come out in the street clear down at the end an' hightailed it at a gallop.'

Casey frowned. 'That's odd.'

'I think he was ridin' that big bay mare.'

'What bay mare?'

'Remember the one with the ear that lopped over sorta funny?'

'Oh, yeah. Good horse. But why would O'Toole be ridin' her? She's a Two-Bar horse.'

The packet of letters forgotten in his hand, Ian said, 'Let's go talk to Mulkey.'

Five minutes later they accosted the stable hand behind the livery barn. 'Hey, Harvey, did O'Toole have a horse put up here?'

Mulkey looked around as if he were suddenly put in a place he didn't want to be. He turned his head and spat a brown stream, then wiped his mouth with the back of his hand. 'Might've,' he evaded.

'Big bay mare?'

'Mighta been.'

'What brand did she have?'

Mulkey scratched the side of his nose. He glanced all around again. 'C-Bar-I, if I remember.'

'You'd remember,' Casey retorted. 'You ain't never failed to notice a brand since I've known you. Anything odd about it?'

For the third time Mulkey looked all around, as if assuring himself nobody else was listening. He spat again, and

197

once more wiped his hand across his mouth. 'Mighty thick bar,' he said finally.

'Whatd'ya mean?'

'I mean the bar 'tween the C an' the I was awful thick.' He held his thumb and finger almost two inches apart. 'Pertneart that thick, as a matter o' fact.'

'Like maybe he blurred the Two-Bar into one really wide bar and added the C and the I?'

Mulkey went through the same routine again before saying, 'Coulda been, all right.'

'Why C-Bar-I?'

'That's his place.'

'O'Toole's place? He owns a ranch?'

'Seems that way. Leastways, most o' the stock he ships outa here seems to have that brand. Some looks a bit shaky, but that brand all right enough.'

'He ships stock out of Chugwater?'

'Outa Chugwater, an' outa Horse Crick, an' outa Slater's, accordin' to what I've heard tell. Don't rightly know how he can have enough cattle or horses either one to run a place, what with all he's sold an' shipped out.'

'Where does he get that much stock to sell?'

'I guess you'll have to ask him about that. I sure ain't gettin' in the middle of it. Now if you boys don't mind, I got a lot o' work to do here.'

He pointedly turned his back on them and began gathering a pitchfork load of hay from a loose stack.

Ian and Casey stood there staring at each other for a long moment. It was Casey who said, 'Maybe we'd best have a talk with Lem, then head out to the Two-Bar.'

'You read my mind,' Ian agreed. 'I do believe horse stealin' is a crime.'

Both had the sinking feeling as they walked toward the marshal's office that the lid was just about to blow off the whole area.

17

'What can I do for you boys? I'd think you'd stirred up enough trouble in town for a while.'

Ian pushed his hat to the back of his head and Casey hooked his thumbs in the front of his belt. It was Casey who said, 'Do you have any authority outside o' town, Lem?'

Lemuel Claude shook his head vigorously enough the ends of his oversized mustache flopped back and forth. 'Nope. He does, though.' He inclined his head toward a man neither Casey nor Ian had noticed, lounging on a chair leaned back against the far wall of Claude's office.

Both Ian and Casey looked back and forth between the town marshal and the stranger, waiting for some sort of explanation. The stranger stood up in a long, fluid motion that put him right in front of the pair. He thrust out a hand. 'The name's Will Hatfield. And you boys are . . . ?'

Ian took the offered hand and gripped it, looking hard into the other's eyes. 'Ian Hennessy.'

Hatfield nodded curtly. 'Heard o' you.'

He turned to Casey and again offered his hand. Casey shook hands with him and said, 'Casey Forester.'

'The bronc busters.'

Both men nodded mutely.

'And sometimes gunfighters,' Hatfield added, in a tone that was at least challenging.

Casey merely returned the man's stare. Ian shook his head. 'Not by choice.'

Hatfield stared back at him a moment that wasn't nearly as long as it seemed to Ian. Then he nodded once, decisively. 'That's the way I've heard it, too. What can I do for you boys?'

Casey responded first. 'Who are you? Aside from someone named Will

Hatfield, that is.'

Hatfield grinned. 'Fair question.' He fished a badge out of his pocket. 'I don't make a habit o' wearin' this thing, but I got it. I'm a Deputy United States Marshal. I was sent up here to look into reports of a whole lot o' cattle rustlin' an' horse stealin'.'

'We arrested the cattle buyer earlier today,' Lem announced.

Both Casey and Ian jerked their heads around and squinted toward the darker end of the marshal's office. Behind the bars of the single cell they could dimly see someone sprawled on one of the two bunks the cell afforded.

'What for?'

'Dealin' in stolen cows. Bunch o' Rafter L stock. The boys sellin' 'em had a bill o' sale that was as bogus as a three-dollar bill. I know Vic Beauchamp, an' it sure as sin wasn't his signature on that paper.'

'Did you arrest the guys who sold 'em to him?'

The marshal shook his head. 'They

were long gone afore we noticed another bunch in the loadin' pens. We was just sittin' here chinnin', tryin' to figure out where that bunch o' thieves is holed up, an' who's runnin' the show.'

Ian and Casey exchanged a meaningful glance. Ian spoke. 'Well, we break horses . . . '

'Yeah, we knowed that.'

'Well, I spotted one o' the horses we broke for the Two-Bar a while ago. We talked to Mulkey — '

'He's the stable hand at the livery barn,' Lem explained to Hatfield.

Ian continued as if he hadn't been interrupted. 'He told us that the horse was branded C-Bar-I.'

'Bennett's outfit,' Lem supplied.

'Yeah, but the bar between the C and the I was wide enough to be called a box, that blurred.'

Silence filled every corner of the room. It was Hatfield who broke it finally. 'And you know this horse?'

'I know every horse I've broken.'

'And you know it's really a Two-Bar horse?'

'Plumb positive.'

Hatfield turned toward the town marshal. 'Where's this Bennett place?'

Lem waved a hand dismissively in the general direction of the mountains to the west. 'It's a good day, day and a half ride over into the mountains.'

'What do you know about Bennett?'

'Well, I know for certain sure he wouldn't be mixed up with no rustlin' deal. On the other hand, I don't recall seein' him an' his missus in town for . . . danged if I remember the last time I talked to 'em. They never did come to town very often. Always stayed overnight o' course. Sometimes a couple or three days, just visitin' folks. Then they'd go back out to the place, an' nobody'd hear from 'em till they showed up in town the next time.'

'What about their hands? I'm guessin' they had some cowboys workin' for 'em.'

Lem nodded. 'Usually three or four.

Cowpokes move around, though, as a rule. Work steady for one outfit a while, draw their time, come to town, stay drunk till the Silver Dollar and the doves o' the roost over there got all their money, then they go back to work for the first rancher that comes to town lookin' for hands.'

'So for all you know, these Bennetts might've sold out to whoever's usin' the place as a hideout?'

Lem thought it over for a long moment. There was an edge of foreboding in his voice when he said, 'I can't imagine them sellin' out. Not by choice. If they had, or if they'd been forced out, they'd have found a way to get to town an' say their goodbyes to folks here. They got a lot o' friends in town. And whoever was workin' for 'em at the time would've drawed their time an' showed up in town.'

'Do they have family?'

The marshal shook his head. 'Nope. None at all. No kids. Well, they had one son. They thought the sun rose and set in that boy. They figured he'd marry most any day, and take over the ranch. Even built a house for him an' the wife they expected him to have. Then he went an' got drowned in a flash flood. Aside from him, they had no other relatives. Oh, Curt told me once that somewheres back East there might be someone that's somehow distantly related to one or the other of 'em, but they didn't actually know of anyone.'

Hatfield's voice was distant. 'All alone in the world, with a ranch pretty isolated in the edge of the mountains,' he mused aloud.

'Seems likely enough to take a ride out there and ask a few questions,' Lem opined.

'You'd best take a bunch o' good men along with you, then,' Ian interjected. 'The ones we've run into from there, and the ones I know from back in Sioux City, wouldn't hesitate to shoot anyone on sight that they thought was a threat.'

Hatfield looked meaningfully at the marshal. Claude stared thoughtfully into space for a long moment. Finally he said, 'Well, O'Grady, that black cowboy from the Diamond J is over at the Silver Dollar. Come to think of it, Billy Feely's with him. Tub Lemke's there too. Him an' another guy come along trailin' them cows the buyer was about to ship. He's workin' for the Rafter L nowadays. One o' the boys from the Flyin' O is there. So's Brick Ferguson from the Two-Bar. That oughta be a-plenty. If we send them out to each o' them ranches with word to bring along everybody they got, we'd end up with maybe thirty men. That'd sure be enough to clean out any rattlesnake's den that's up there.'

Silence once again filled the place, seeping into all the corners, leaving the squeaking of the marshal's chair as the only sound. It was Casey who said, 'You won't wanta go bustin' in up there without knowin' the lay o' things. How about if me'n Ian ride on up there, kinda quiet like, an' look things over? Then we can meet you somewhere and let you know what's what.'

The two lawmen exchanged a look of enquiry that quickly turned into a look of agreement. 'Well, keep your heads down. No sense you boys gettin' yourselves killed. Three days from now, long about mid-morning, we'll meet up with you at the big spring at the head of Richeu Crick. We'll have the boys from the other ranches meet us at the Rafter L, so we can gather there. That's the closest one to Bennett's place. If we pull outa there ahead o' sunup, we can be to the springs by mid-morning easy.'

Ian and Casey both nodded. Lacking anything else to say, they turned and walked out of the marshal's office. They stopped on the sidewalk. As they looked back and forth along the main street of Chugwater, both wondered if they would ever see the town again.

Ian suddenly remembered the packet of letters in his pocket. He was overwhelmed with an urgency to read them. Then another thought struck him. 'I 'spect I'd best get a letter sent off to Corky,' he said. 'Just in case I don't get the chance again.'

Casey took a deep breath. 'Yeah. I gotta let Iva know what's goin' on, too. Meet you at the livery barn in a couple hours?'

'Yeah,' was all Ian said, but he felt as if he had to force the word out through a pressing cloud of doom. What would he put in a letter that might be his last message to the woman he loved? He had the sudden premonition that it would be the very last thing she would ever hear from him.

18

It was quiet. It was too quiet. Even the birds seemed frozen in place, lest they stir a leaf or a branch and break the profound silence.

Sitting in the finger of blue spruce that jutted into the flat valley, they watched the approaching bunch of cattle from nearly a mile away. Dust rose in the air behind their hoofs, then drifted slowly away in the quiet air. Even from that distance, they would have heard if the pair driving the cows were using their voices to goad the placid bovines forward. There was no need. They smelled water, and they were thirsty.

Ian and Casey watched silently. Less than a hundred feet from their place of concealment, a spring formed a pool of water. It turned into a trickling stream possibly 200 yards long, before it slipped out of sight in a small rocky defile. Chances were it would reappear lower on the mountain, and join with other rivulets to form a mountain stream. Here it only provided a welcome respite from the arid trek the cattle had obviously been compelled to make.

The two drovers rode away from the small herd, giving their horses their heads, allowing them to trot to the welcome respite the spring promised. As they did, a few of the cows broke into a trot toward the water as well. Most just picked up the pace of their walk, heads thrust forward, savoring the promise the smell of water in the air provided.

Ian and Casey should have been visible, where they sat their horses, had the other pair been as alert as their chosen profession demanded. Instead they began to exchange small talk obliviously.

'We takin' this bunch on down to the Horse Crick pens?'

'Nah. For some reason Shaun wants to keep 'em up around the place for a while.'

'That ain't smart. There ain't no way to change a Diamond J brand to a C-Bar-I.'

'Who's gonna see 'em anyway?'

'Somebody could come along.'

'Not likely. He'll have a bill o' sale for 'em whenever we move 'em on down to the railroad.'

'Yeah, I s'pose. I don't like him hangin' on to all the money from everythin' we been sellin', though.'

The other gave a short, hard laugh. 'You don't trust Shaun?'

'Do you?'

'I've known 'im way too long to trust 'im as far as I can throw a bull.'

'So how come you're lettin' him hang on to all your money too?'

'I'll get what's comin' to me when I'm ready to light outa this country,' the other blustered.

'Or a chunk o' hot lead for askin',' the other rejoined. 'You've known the

212

boss longer'n any of us. Do you think he's ever gonna divvy up the money?'

A long silence ensued while they both emptied their canteens and refilled them with the ice-cold spring water. There was a distinct uncertainty in the other's voice when he said, 'Well, I have known him a long time. Since we was kids, actually.'

'Yeah, back in Sioux City,' answered a voice from the timber unexpectedly.

Both men cursed explosively and jerked their guns from their holsters. Both fired blindly into the trees, spotting Ian and Casey after they had begun pulling the triggers. Their shots had no more effect than ripping small branches from the trees.

The roar of Ian and Casey's .45s issued precisely together. Both of the rustlers grunted and took a step backward. One flopped on to his back and lay still, arms spread-eagled, his gun forgotten as it flew from his dead hand.

The other sat down abruptly and looked at the pair who had shot them as if trying to understand something that remained just beyond his ability to grasp.

As Casey and Ian walked forward, guns in hand, he frowned. 'Ian?' he said.

'Stan,' Ian acknowledged with a single word.

'I, I ain't gonna fight ya no more,' Stan said, confusion evident in his voice. 'I'm whipped.'

'What brought you clear out here, Stan?' Ian asked, more as an expression of sorrow and remorse than an actual question.

'It was Shaun, you know,' Stan said, as if explaining something Ian should have known. 'It was always Shaun. He always told us what to do.'

'He's the one leadin' the rustlin' ring?' Ian offered, half rhetorically.

'He's always the one leadin',' Stan explained, still clearly puzzled that Ian didn't seem to understand that.

'What happened to the Bennetts?' Ian demanded.

'Who?'

'The Bennetts? The couple that own the C-Bar-I.'

'Oh. Them. Shaun, he — '

His words were interrupted by a sudden gush of blood that issued from his mouth. He choked on it for just a moment. His eyes opened wide in silent appeal for Ian to do something, anything. Then they glazed over. He fell over sideways. Blood continued to trickle from the side of his mouth, making a dark stain on the grass.

It was impossible for either Ian or Casey to talk for a full minute. As it almost always was, it was Casey who broke the silence. 'Another of your old school chums from Iowa?'

Ian took a deep, ragged breath. 'Yeah. I can't believe Shaun could get all three of 'em to come along with him all the way out here, and set up a deal like he's got goin' here. They had to know they'd get caught, sooner or later.'

'At least O'Toole should have known that.'

Ian was thoughtful for a long moment. 'I'm guessin' he does. I'm guessin' he has it planned to bleed it for all it's worth, hang on to everybody's money, and quit the country when he figures they're about to get caught. He'll leave all the others behind to face the music.'

'Is he that smart?'

'Yeah, he's that smart.'

'Is he that much of a double-crosser? Even outlaws sorta take care o' their friends.'

'Shaunnessy O'Toole only has one friend: Shaunnessy O'Toole.'

'Is he really that bad?'

'He's all o' that bad.'

'In that case, we'd best watch our backs. He mighta heard them shots from here. We ain't that far from the Bennetts' place.'

Even as Casey said the words, a chill of premonition crawled its way up Ian's back.

19

'He's got more of a crew than I expected.'

Casey's whisper was barely adequate to reach Ian's ear. They lay on a low hill overlooking the yard of the C-Bar-I ranch.

'Less than he did have,' Ian observed.

Most of the ranch yard looked like a hundred others scattered over the Wyoming landscape. The ranch house itself had begun as little more than a log shack, then been added to and improved as prosperous times permitted. Over time it had become a comfortable house, with a long porch that wrapped around two sides. A pair of old chairs sat side by side, facing the stunning view the ranch's position on the side of the mountain afforded. It was apparent the owners spent a lot of time sitting there together, enjoying each other and the prosperity they had earned so dearly.

The bunkhouse was small, as ranches go. It appeared to have room for half a dozen hands at most. There was no cookhouse, making it apparent that their hands ate at their table. That, in itself, was unusual. Most ranchers, even those who treated their hands well, considered them of a different breed, and unworthy of eating with family. Some regarded them as having less value than a good horse.

The barn was not pretentious, but it was more than adequate for the needs of a ranch that size.

There were two other things that made the ranch yard distinctively different from most others: one was the second house, spaced just far enough from the main house for privacy, facing the same splendid view enjoyed by the other house — obviously the house built for the son who didn't live to enjoy it. The other was the cemetery plot. Almost all ranches had their own burial place. It was a hard country and a hard life, and more than a few cowboys, as well as their bosses, lost their lives to blizzards, rustlers, Indians, flash floods, angry cows, an awkward landing from being bucked off a horse, or a hundred other hazards that were an everyday part of life. Almost always the deceased was wrapped in a blanket and buried there on the place.

What was unusual was the size of the cemetery on the C-Bar-I.

One grave was surrounded by a carefully built fence. Hardy perennial flowers bloomed around it where they had been carefully and lovingly planted. There was no doubt it was the grave of that son.

Half a dozen other graves were not at all distinctive. What was strange was nine relatively new graves. None of them had even weeds growing on them. They were recent.

'Lotta graves,' Casey noted.

'The others oughta be here any time.'

'Maybe we shoulda stayed with them.'

Ian shook his head. 'I wanted to be where we could see what happens when they know they're caught up with. We got a real good view from here.'

They had met up with the posse led by Hatfield and Claude as planned. They had filled them in on what they had learned, and on their killing of two of the rustlers. Then they had asked for time to circle around so they could command their present vantage point.

Abruptly a voice from the timber, a hundred yards from the house, yelled out, 'Everybody on the place, come out in the open with your hands in the air. This is the United States Marshal, and we have a posse of thirty-three men surrounding you. Come out with your hands up.'

Deathly silence followed the words for several heartbeats. Then the serenity of the day was shattered with a fusillade of gunfire from the windows of both the bunkhouse and the main house. It was answered by thirty-three guns pouring lead back at those windows.

Suddenly the back door of the main house burst open. Shaunnessy O'Toole broke from the house, running bent over, firing at the puffs of smoke from the assaulting fire as he ran. He ducked into the barn, seemingly unharmed.

Moments later he raced out of the barn astride the big bay mare Ian had noted in town. At a dead run he spurred the horse on a path that would bring him within a few yards of Ian and Casey, and slightly below them.

He managed, somehow, to speed unscathed through the hail of gunfire directed at him, until trees screened him from the posse. When he was almost even with them, Ian and Casey stood. 'Far enough, Shaun!' Ian yelled.

As if expecting their presence, Shaun instantly responded, sending three rapid shots their way, while flopping forward on to the horse's neck and jamming his spurs into its sides. The horse lunged forward. Ian's shot missed. Casey grunted.

Ian's eyes darted to his friend. Casey

looked stunned. He gripped his abdomen near the right side. Blood was already seeping out between his fingers. 'You're hit!' Ian explained.

'Not bad,' Casey insisted. 'Go after him. Don't let 'im get away.'

'I can't leave you like this!'

'Go! I'll be fine. Don't let him get away.'

Impossibly torn, Ian's eyes darted toward where Shaun had disappeared in the trees, then back to his friend, then back again toward his fleeing enemy, then back at Casey, back and forth, back and forth.

'Go!' Casey yelled at him.

Finally he did. He sprinted to his horse and leaped into the saddle. He threw caution to the winds, determined to catch the nemesis who had haunted his life for so many years.

The path of the fleeing outlaw was easy to follow. The running horse left deep prints in the soft ground, as well as a trail of broken twigs and branches of trees to mark its path.

For nearly a-quarter mile Ian followed at full speed. Then he began to notice a change in the trail. The hoofprints were suddenly not so deep. Fewer broken branches marked the path. Then there were none at all.

'He slowed down,' Ian breathed. 'He's headin' for somewhere special.'

Watching intently, he slowed his own horse. He was about to top a low rise covered with new-growth spruce trees when a small sound caused him to jerk his horse to a halt. He dismounted and crept forward on foot, working his way silently through the small trees, most no more than eight or ten feet tall.

He spotted Shaun's horse first. She was standing, reins dragging the ground, waiting patiently as Ian had taught her to do when the reins were dropped on the ground.

Slipping forward as quietly as possible, he soon spotted Shaun as well. He had moved a large, flat rock that few men could have moved unaided. He was bent over, retrieving wrapped packages from a hole that had been fashioned beneath the stone.

Ian walked forward silently until he was about twenty feet behind Shaun. 'So this is where you kept the money hid from the others,' he said quietly.

Instead of whirling, gun in hand, as Ian expected, Shaun froze for a long moment. He stood up slowly. Hands away from his body, he turned just as slowly around to face the man less than half his size, who had been, in his mind, the biggest problem in his life. Ian could feel the virulent hatred emanating from the big man as he glared at him.

'Managed to follow me, huh?'

'It wasn't all that hard.'

'You been makin' my life miserable since the sixth reader.'

'Nobody's fault but yours. You're just gonna leave all your men to face the music alone, huh?'

Shaun snorted. 'Bunch o' losers. They'll get what they deserve.'

'While you ride away with all the money.'

Shaun grinned unexpectedly, his confidence returning with each breath. 'You got it, little man. Shaunnessy always comes out the winner in the end.'

'What did you do with the Bennetts?'

A shadow crossed Shaun's eyes for the briefest moment. 'They don't matter,' he dismissed.

'They mattered to each other.'

Shaun shrugged. 'So they got to walk the dead path together.'

'You shot them.' It was a statement, not a question.

Shaun grinned again. 'I didn't enjoy it, though. Not near as much as I enjoyed shootin' that show-off horse o' yours.'

He expected the announcement to disrupt Ian's concentration, to upset him, to distract him just enough to allow him to beat the smaller man to the draw. The words had the desired effect of hitting Ian like a blow. It wasn't nearly enough. His training was too good, too thorough. His reflexes had been too tightly honed by the hours of practice.

Shaun's gun was just clearing leather when Ian's first bullet slammed into his chest, driving him backward. He continued his draw anyway, bringing his gun to bear on his despised enemy. Ian's second shot slammed into him, driving him back another step. The gun in his hand wavered, then lifted again. A third shot from Ian's gun seemed to have no effect. With dogged determination the big man brought his gun to bear directly on Ian's chest. Ian's fourth bullet shattered his right shoulder, causing the shot he managed to fire to go just wide, missing Ian by an inch.

With a mighty effort Shaun managed to fire a second time, but the shattered shoulder refused to align the gun, and it fired harmlessly into the ground. Still glaring malevolently at Ian, he dropped to his knees. Finally, then, his eyes wavered and went blank. He fell forward on to his face.

Without taking his eyes from the

dead man, Ian thumbed out the spent brass from his .45 and replaced them with fresh cartridges. Aloud he breathed, 'Four shots. Three in the chest, then I busted his shoulder, and he still managed to get off two shots. Whatever else he was, he was one tough Irishman.'

A sense of something that had shadowed him from long ago and far away lifted suddenly, leaving him weak-kneed and trembling. He felt suddenly as if he were free, really free, for the first time in his life.

He holstered his gun and walked over to finish the job of stuffing the packages of money into the two sets of saddle-bags that the dead man had begun. In the distance, the sounds of gunfire had suddenly fallen silent.

'That must mean they gave up,' he guessed. 'It's finally over.'

Epilogue

When Ian made his way back to the C-Bar-I ranch yard, three rustlers were laid out on the ground by the small cemetery. Five others still swung slowly from the limbs of the closest trees. Some of the posse were already busy digging the graves to dispose of the bodies.

Casey was with the posse, his wound adjudged to not be at all life-threatening, even though he wasn't going to be breaking any horses for a while. He opined that Iva would delight in taking really good care of him. Right after the wedding.

Each of the area ranchers estimated the number of cattle and horses they had lost to the rustling ring, and were repaid for their value from the money Ian had recovered. When it was all said and done, there was a good bit of money unaccounted for.

The ranchers and lawmen present for that meeting discussed that problem and arrived at a solution that seemed agreeable to all present.

Since the Bennetts were both dead and without heirs, the deputy US marshal suggested he would be able to have a quitclaim deed issued to either Ian or Casey. At both men's insistence it was determined to issue the deed in their names jointly. Thus the two became instant owners of the C-Bar-I ranch. They flipped a coin to decide which one got the main house, and which one got the house that had been built for the Bennetts' son.

Ian took the first train East to Sioux City to claim his bride. He actually arrived there on the same train that bore his letter explaining all that had happened. For that reason, there was nobody at the station to greet him. Corky more than made up for that disappointment when he showed up at her family's home.

Should you happen to be riding along the front range of the Iron Mountains, south and west of Chugwater, Wyoming, you might stop in at a place called the C-Bar-I, or the C-I, as the locals call it. You'll find it one of the most pleasant visits you could imagine. Fat cattle graze the mountainsides. The most beautiful and well-trained horses in the country come from there these days.

It's a bit of a chore to sort out which of the children running about wear the name of Hennessy and which are Foresters. There seems to be an abundance of both.

Not one among them seems the least bit afraid of anything, or anyone.

THE END

We do hope that you have enjoyed reading this large print book.

Did you know that all of our titles are available for purchase?

We publish a wide range of high quality large print books including:
Romances, Mysteries, Classics
General Fiction
Non Fiction and Westerns

Special interest titles available in large print are:
The Little Oxford Dictionary
Music Book, Song Book
Hymn Book, Service Book

Also available from us courtesy of Oxford University Press:
Young Readers' Dictionary
(large print edition)
Young Readers' Thesaurus
(large print edition)

For further information or a free brochure, please contact us at:
Ulverscroft Large Print Books Ltd.,
The Green, Bradgate Road, Anstey,
Leicester, LE7 7FU, England.
Tel: (00 44) **0116 236 4325**
Fax: (00 44) **0116 234 0205**

Other titles in the
Linford Western Library:

THE HOT SPURS

Boyd Cassidy

When the riders of the Bar 10 run up against an escaped prisoner and his ruthless gang, they find themselves in deep trouble. Bret Jarvis and his henchmen are heading to Mexico, where men of the Circle J ranch have returned from a profitable cattle drive — making them sitting targets for a raid. But Gene Adams and his Bar 10 cowboys are soon in hot pursuit — all they need to do is stop the outlaws before they reach the border . . .

LONG RIDIN' MAN

Jake Douglas

They call him 'Hunter'. There is one man in particular for whom he searches: the man who destroyed his family. Trailing the killer, Hunter finds himself in a booming town short of one deputy sheriff: in need of cash, he pins on the badge. But the folk of Cimarron begin to wonder just who they've hired as their peacemaker. Once Hunter discovers why the town needed a fast gun so urgently, the odds are that it will be too late for him to get out alive . . .

POWDER RIVER

Jack Edwardes

As the State Governor's lawmen spread throughout Wyoming, the days of the bounty hunter are coming to a close. For hired gun Brad Thornton, this spells the end of an era. The men in badges aren't yet everywhere, though, and rancher Moreton Frewen needs immediate action: rustlers are stealing his stock, and Thornton is just the man to make the culprits pay. But these are no run-of-the-mill cattle thieves. The Morgan gang are ruthless killers, prepared to turn their hands to anything from bank robbery to murder . . .